KB269961

세계의 위대한 지도자들

Great Leaders of the World

DARAKWON

About Wise & Wide

- 렉사일 지수(Lexile® measures)에 맞춘 체계적인 6단계 영어 독서 프로그램
- 우리나라와 세계의 초등 교과 과정을 분석해 뽑은 다채롭고 흥미로운 주제
- 스토리, 설명문, 명작 리라이팅 등 다양한 형식의 새롭고 유익한 읽을거리
- 정보와 재미, 논픽션 학습과 픽션 학습의 장점을 한 번에!
- 탄탄한 독후 활동으로 쑥쑥 자라는 사고력

Wise & Wide는 렉사일 지수(Lexile® measures)를 기준으로 각 단계를 체계적으로 나눈, 총 60권 구성의 6단계 영어 독서 프로그램입니다. 렉사일 지수는 미국 정규 공교육 과정과 여러 영어 프로그램에서 가장 많이 사용되는 영어 독서 지수입니다. 미국 50개 주 가운데 21개 주에서 렉사일 지수를 학기말 시험(End of Grade) 성적표에 직접 표시하며, 세계적으로 저명한 300개 이상의 출판사들이 렉사일 지수를 채택하여 사용하고 있기도 합니다. 우리나라와 미국, 영국, 호주 등 세계 초등 교과 과정을 분석해 뽑은 흥미로운 주제로 미국, 영국의 우수한 작가들이 집필한 다양한 종류의 읽을거리를 만나보세요. 도표(organizer) 완성, 자기 생각 말하기, 독후 테스트 풀기 등 탄탄한 독후 활동도 준비되어 있습니다.

시리즈 수준 & 렉사일 지수

시리즈 단계	렉사일 지수	미국 학년 (U.S. Grade)
Level 1	200L 이하	Pre K - K
Level 2	190L - 400L	Lower Grade 1
Level 3	350L - 530L	Upper Grade 1
Level 4	420L - 650L	Grade 2
Level 5	520L - 940L	Grade 3 - 4
Level 6	830L - 1070L	Grade 5 - 6

* 똑똑한 영어 읽기 Wise & Wide 시리즈의 1단계는 미국의 미취학 수준에 해당합니다.

* 렉사일 지수와 미국 학년과의 관계 출처: CCSS(Common Core State Standards) FOR ENGLISH LANGUAGE ARTS, APPENDIX A (2012, 미국 45개 주에서 사용 중)

퍼즐처럼 다양한 Topic List

	Level 1	Level 2	Level 3	Level 4	Level 5	Level 6
1권	과학〉생물: 동물들의 겨울잠 Story	과학〉생물: 생물과 무생물 Story	과학〉생물〉 동물, 환경: 해달 Story	환경〉 자연과 인생: 해녀 & 감나무 Story	과학〉생물〉 동물: 아마존의 놀라운 동물들 Story	과학〉생물: 세균, 전염성 질환 Story
2권	문학〉세계 명작: 이솝 우화 Story	문학〉전래 동화: 돌에 관한 옛이야기 Story	사회〉경제: 용돈 버는 사업, 저축 Story	과학〉생물〉 식물: 광합성 Story	과학〉지구과학: 지각, 지진, 화산, 대기 Report	수학〉수열: 황금 비율과 피보나치 수열 Story
3권	과학〉물리: 그림자의 원리 Story	문학〉세계 명작: 피터 팬 Story	과학〉과학 기술: 나노봇 Story	문학〉신화: 세계의 천지 창조 이야기 Story	문학〉전설: 아서왕 이야기 Story	문학〉신화: 별자리 신화 Story
4권	문학〉전래 문학: 탈무드 Story	과학〉생물〉 동물: 북극곰 Story	과학〉생물〉 동물: 마운틴 고릴라 Story	사회〉인류 문화: 세계의 놀라운 고대 문화 Story	과학〉지구과학: 구름과 날씨 Story	문학〉 인간과 동물: 소녀와 말의 우정 Story
5권	사회〉윤리: 생활 속의 규범 Story	과학〉생물: 몸의 감각 Report	사회〉인류 문화: 세계의 독특한 축제 Report	예술〉음악: 오페라 이야기 Story	사회〉세계 문화· 역사: 르네상스 시대의 특징 Story	스포츠〉 보드 스포츠: 서핑 & 스노보딩 Story
6권	사회〉세계지리, 여행: 세계의 명소 Story	과학〉생물〉 동물: 공룡 Story	과학〉천문학: 우주, 태양계 행성 Story	사회〉인물: 고난을 이겨낸 세 위인들 Story	과학〉과학 기술: 놀라운 로봇의 세계 Report	예술〉음악: 낭만주의 시대의 작곡가들 Report
7권	과학〉우주 과학: 우주 비행사들의 생활 Report	사회〉인류 문화: 세계의 전설 속 괴물들 Report	수학〉기초 수학: 숫자, 측정, 형태, 데이터 Report	과학·사회〉 기술, 문화: 세계의 발명품 Report	예술〉미술: 세계의 명화 Report	사회〉인간과 동물: 인간을 위해 활약 하는 동물들 Report
8권	사회〉인류 문화: 세계의 다양한 생활 문화 Story	예술〉음악: 오케스트라의 악기들 Story	사회〉생활 안전: 조난 시 기본 대처 방법 Story	사회〉역사: 미국의 골드러시 Report	사회·과학〉 심리학: 생활 속의 심리학 Story	문학〉세계 명작: 베니스의 상인 Story
9권	사회〉직업: 여러 직업에 관한 인터뷰 Report	과학〉과학 기술: 시대의 변화와 기술의 발달 Story	사회〉정치〉선거: 학생회장 선거 Story	문학〉세계 명작: 셜록 홈즈 이야기 Story	문학〉세계 명작: 15소년 표류기 Story	사회〉역사·인물: 역사 속의 리더들 Report
10권	문학〉전래 동화: 같은 주제의 동·서양 옛이야기 Story	스포츠〉겨울 스포 츠: 동계 올림픽 종목의 이모저모 Report	문학〉세계 명작: 오 헨리 단편 Story	스포츠〉구기 종목: 인기 있는 구기 종목의 이모저모 Report	사회〉역사: 역사를 뒤바꾼 세계사의 명장면 Report	예술·사회〉미술: 그림의 창작·유통· 보존에 관한 이야기 Report

* 똑똑한 영어 읽기 Wise & Wide 시리즈는 60권까지 계속 출간됩니다.

How to Use This Book

●Before Reading

어떤 분야, 어떤 종류의 이야기를 읽게 될지, 줄거리는 어떠한지 미리 쉽게 알아볼 수 있어요.

●영어 본문

미국, 영국의 우수한 작가들이 집필하여 각 단계의 수준에 맞는 영어 문장·표현의 참맛을 제대로 느낄 수 있어요.

●Pop Quiz

쪽지 시험처럼 핵심을 찌르는 퀴즈로 해당 페이지의 내용을 잘 이해하고 있는지 바로 확인해 보세요.

●어휘 설명

일일이 사전을 찾아보지 않아도 주요 어휘와 표현의 뜻을 알 수 있어요.

●Aha! 상식

Aha! 표시가 붙어 있는 문장에 대한 설명은 여기서 확인하세요. 문화 상식, 영어 구문이나 문법 상식, 그리고 과학·경제 상식까지! 각 분야의 상식들이 알차게 들어 있어 읽는 재미가 두 배예요.

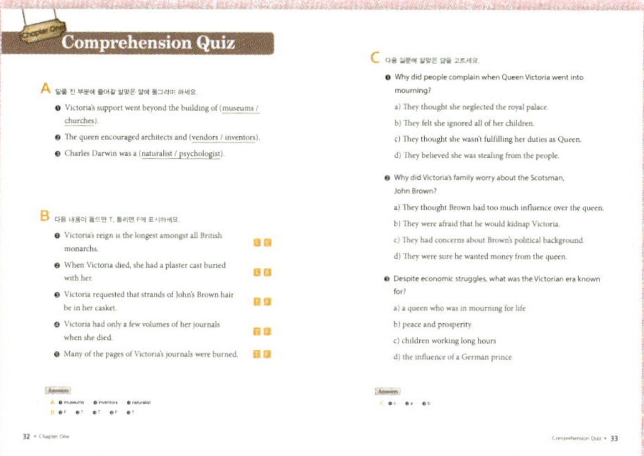

•Comprehension Quiz

한 chapter를 다 읽은 후에는 다양한 문제를 풀어보며 내용을 제대로 이해했는지 정리하고 넘어가세요.

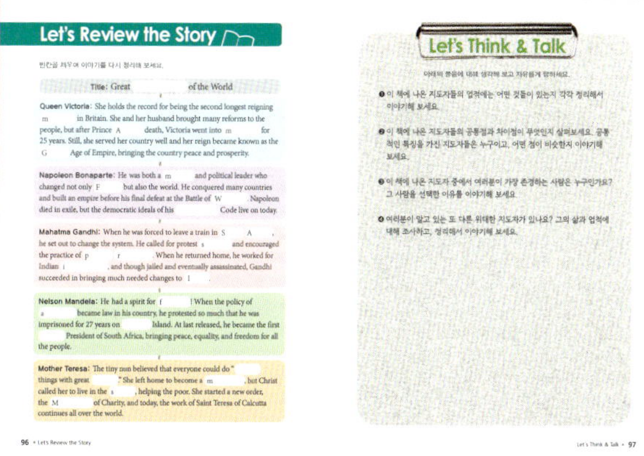

•Let's Review the Story /
•Let's Think & Talk

Organizer의 빈칸을 채우며 전체 이야기를 요약하고, 질문에 답하며 내 생각과 느낌을 자유롭게 정리해 봐요. 훗날 논술에 대비할 논리력과 사고력을 기를 수 있어요.

부록

Audio CD

책의 내용이 그대로 담긴 오디오 CD. 오디오 극장처럼 생생하고 재미있는 음원을 만나보세요. (MP3 파일 PC·모바일 무료 다운로드)

온·오프라인 독후 테스트 & 온라인 단어 퀴즈·단어 리스트

독후 테스트는 책 또는 온라인으로 풀어볼 수 있어요. 온라인으로 풀면 좀 더 자세한 응시 결과와 함께, 전체 응시자들과 비교했을 때 내 실력이 어느 정도 위치인지도 알아볼 수 있어요.

추가로 제공되는 온라인 단어 퀴즈도 풀어보시고, 단어 리스트도 PC나 모바일로 무료로 다운로드 받으세요.

www.darakwon.co.kr

Before Reading

세계의 위대한 지도자들

Level 6–9,
Lexile® 1040L | •사회〉역사·인물
•report

지도자의 진정한 역할과 의미는 무엇일까?

지도자란 무엇일까요? 단순히 한 조직이나 나라를 대표하는 사람으로 그 권력을 자기 이익만을 위해 쓰는 이는 아닐 거예요. 자신이 이끄는 조직의 어려움이나 부조리함을 그 조직의 구성원들을 위해 정의로운 방법으로 변화시키는 힘을 만들어내는 것이 바로 지도자의 역할이 아닐까요? 세계 역사를 들여다보면 다양한 지도자들이 있었어요. 세계를 전쟁과 혼란으로 이끈 악명 높은 지도자가 있었는가 하면, 국내의 경제적 부흥과 사회적 변화를 이끌었을 뿐 아니라 전 세계의 인종 차별과 식민지 제도 철폐를 위해 노력한 이들도 있었고, 어려운 이들을 위해 헌신적으로 봉사하여 주변 사람들을 감동시키며 사회적인 변화를 끌어낸 지도자들도 있었어요.

이 책에서는 세계 근·현대사 속에서 위대한 지도자로 손꼽히는 다섯 명을 살펴볼 거예요. 이들이 어떤 리더십을 발휘해 변화를 끌어냈는지 함께 알아봐요.

줄거리

이 책에서는 세계 역사 속에 등장했던 여러 지도자 가운데 세계 근·현대사 속에서 국내 또는 전 세계에 긍정적인 영향을 주었던 다섯 명의 지도자를 살펴볼 거예요.

먼저, 영국의 빅토리아 여왕은 '해가 지지 않는 나라'라는 대영제국의 최전성기를 통치했으며, 인도 제국에 군림한 최초의 영국 군주이기도 했어요.

프랑스의 대표적인 지도자인 나폴레옹은 군인 신분에서 최고 지도자인 황제 자리에 오른 인물로, 유럽 여러 나라로 프랑스 세력을 확장시켰죠.

인도의 대표적인 정신적 지주인 간디는 비폭력 저항 운동으로 대표되는 활동을 통해 영국으로부터의 인도 독립을 끌어낸 지도자예요.

남아프리카공화국 최초의 흑인 대통령인 넬슨 만델라는 1950년대 당시 남아프리카공화국에 존재했던 불평등한 인종 차별 정책에 저항해 흑인의 인권을 위해 활동했어요.

마더 테레사는 나라를 직접 통치한 지도자는 아니었지만 평생을 가난하고 소외당하는 이들과 함께하며 그들에게 봉사한 인류의 정신적 지도자였죠.

Contents

Great Leaders of the World

세계의 위대한 지도자들

세계의 위대한 지도자들

Great Leaders of the World

What Makes a Great Leader?

무엇이 위대한 지도자를 만드는가?

If you were asked to name the world's greatest leader from the eighteenth, nineteenth, or twentieth centuries, who would you say? Would you choose a political ruler, a king, a queen, or an emperor? Or perhaps you'd select a humanitarian, an industrial pioneer, a global inventor, or even a spiritual guide. But whomever you picked, you'd probably find that your choice for a great leader had many traits in common with those chosen by others.

Great leaders tend to have similar characteristics. They are often ambitious and confident, and yet still have a humble and compassionate nature. They are visionaries; that is, they see the future creatively. Expect to also find courage in a great leader, though not always the kind of courage that would lead troops into battle. And don't forget persistence. These are men and women who refuse to quit, despite the odds stacked against them!

- **name** 이름을 밝히다, 명명하다; 이름
- **ruler** 통치자, 지배자
- **emperor** 황제
- **select** 고르다, 선택하다
- **humanitarian** 인도주의자; 인도주의의
- **industrial** 산업의, 실업의
- **pioneer** 선구자, 개척자
- **spiritual** 정신적인, 종교적인
- **whomever** 누구든지
- **trait** 특성, 특징
- **in common with** ~와 같은, ~와 마찬가지로
- **tend to + 동사원형** ~하는 경향이 있다
- **characteristic** 특징, 특질; 특징적인
- **ambitious** 야심 찬, 야망을 품은
- **confident** 자신감 있는, 확신하는
- **and yet** 그렇다 하더라도, 그럼에도 불구하고
- **humble** 겸손한, 소박한
- **compassionate** 동정심이 있는, 인정 많은
- **nature** 본성, 천성, 자연
- **visionary** 선지자; 예지력 있는
- **that is** 즉, 말하자면
- **expect to + 동사원형** ~하기를 기대하다
- **the kind of** 이 같은
- **troop** 병력, 군대
- **persistence** 불굴, 끈기, 고집
- **refuse** 거부하다, 거절하다
- **quit** 그만두다, 중지하다
- **despite** ~에도 불구하고
- **odds** 역경, 곤란, (어떤 일이 있을) 가능성
- **stack against** ~에게 불리하게 조작하다

Aha! English

But whomever you picked, you'd probably find ~. 하지만 여러분이 <u>누구를</u> <u>뽑든지</u>, 여러분은 아마도 ~ 발견할 것이다.

whomever는 '복합관계대명사'로, whoever, whatever처럼 '관계대명사 + ever'의 형태로 써요. 의미는 관계대명사 고유의 의미에 '~든지'가 더해져서 '누구든지(whomever), 무엇이든지(whatever)' 등이 돼요.

ex Give it to <u>whomever</u> you like. <u>누구든</u> 네가 좋아하는 사람한테 그것을 주어라.

Great leaders are trailblazers, teachers, and thinkers, and
though they may have their faults, they will always leave the
world a better place for future generations.

Thankfully, there have been many great recent leaders who
have changed the world for the better, so it would indeed be
difficult to name just one. Instead, let's take a closer look at
five leaders from the last few centuries. After learning about a
long-lived queen, a tenacious emperor, a surprising protester,
a passionate president, and one very tiny nun, see if you can
name the qualities that they all share!

- **trailblazer** 선구자, 개척자
- **thinker** 사상가, 생각하는 사람
- **fault** 단점, 결함
- **leave** (어떤 상태가) 되게 하다,
  ~한 상태로 놓아 두다(leave-left-left)
- **generation** 세대
- **thankfully** 고맙게도, 다행스럽게도
- **recent** 근대의, 최근의
- **for the better** 보다 나은 쪽으로

- **indeed** 사실, 실제로, 정말
- **instead** 대신에
- **take a look** ~을 보다(take-took-taken)
- **long-lived** 장수하는, 오래가는
- **tenacious** 결연한, 완강한
- **protester** 시위자, 항의자
- **passionate** 열정적인, 열심인
- **nun** 수녀
- **quality** (사람의) 자질, 특성

Aha! English

~, so it would indeed be difficult to name just one. ~, 그래서 딱 한 사람의 이름만 대
는 것은 정말로 어려울 것이다.

이 문장의 진짜 주어는 문장 뒤쪽에 나온 to name just one이에요. 이렇게 to부정사가 주어로 쓰여 주어가
길 때는 원래 주어 자리에 의미가 없는 가짜 주어 it을 쓰고, 진짜 주어인 to부정사는 문장 맨 뒤로 보내요.
ex It was against the law to print photos of him! 그의 사진들을 인쇄하는 것은 법을 어기는 것이었다!

Queen Victoria, a Royal for the Ages

아주 오랫동안 왕족이었던 빅토리아 여왕

In her time, Queen Victoria had the longest reign of any monarch in British history. Even today, she holds the record among all British kings and queens for being the second longest reigning monarch. But her long reign, though notable, is not what made Victoria a great leader. There was much more to this grandmother of a queen than simply all the years she wore the crown!

Almost from infancy, Victoria was destined to be queen. And so her mother, and her mother's confidant, John Conroy, raised her under strict rules. Stifled, she began to keep a diary when she was just thirteen years old. In her journals, Victoria could write and say whatever she liked, a daily habit that she continued up until ten days before she died!

- **royal** 왕족; 국왕[여왕]의
- **for the ages** 아주 오랜 기간 동안; 주목할 만한
  (*cf.* age (역사적으로 특정한) 시대, 나이)
- **in one's time** 살아있는 동안에, ~의 시대에는
- **reign** 통치 기간, 치세; 통치하다
- **monarch** 군주, 제왕
- **hold the record** 기록을 보유하다(*cf.* hold 보유하다,
  잡다, (지위에) 있다(hold-held-held))
- **notable** 주목할 만한, 중요한
- **wear the crown** 왕위에 있다(wear-wore-worn)
  (*cf.* crown 왕위, 왕관, 국왕의 영토; 왕위에 앉히다)

- **infancy** 유아기, 초창기
- **be destined to + 동사원형** ~할 운명이다
- **confidant** (비밀도 털어놓을 정도의) 친구
- **raise** (아이를) 키우다, 들어올리다
- **stifle** 숨 막히게 하다, 억누르다
- **keep a diary** 일기를 쓰다
  (keep-kept-kept)
- **journal** 일기, 저널
- **habit** 습관, (수도사나 수녀가 입는) 의복
- **up until** ~에 이르기까지(until의 강조형)

When, at the young age of eighteen, she took the throne, Victoria immediately asserted her own will. She sent her mother to live in rooms on the far side of the palace. And as for her mother's friend, John Conroy, she banned him from her life, never seeing him again. Instead, she relied upon her prime minister, Lord Melbourne, to advise and teach her.

The support of the British population for the crown was at an all-time low at the time of Victoria's coronation, and so the new queen had her work cut out for her. Though she made mistakes in the early days, young Victoria, with the steady help of Lord Melbourne, gradually learned what it was to be a monarch. And in doing so, she won the trust of her people.

ⓑ 답정

- **take the throne** 왕위에 오르다
- **assert** 주장하다, 확고히 하다
- **will** 의지, (강한) 의견, 유언장; ~일 것이다
- **on the far side of** ~의 저쪽에
  (*cf.* far 가장 멀리에 있는; 훨씬, 멀리)
- **as for** ~에 대해 말하자면
- **ban** 금지하다; 금지
- **rely upon** ~에 의지하다
- **prime minister** 수상(*cf.* minister 장관)
- **Lord** (영국에서 귀족을 칭하는) 경

- **support** 지지, 지원; 지지하다
- **population** 주민, 인구
- **all-time low** 지금까지 제일 낮은 수준
- **coronation** 대관식
- **have one's work cut out (for one)** 매우 고생하다, 애먹다, 아주 바쁘다(have-had-had)
- **steady** 꾸준한, 한결같은
- **gradually** 점점, 서서히
- **in doing so** 그렇게 하면서
- **win** (노력을 통해) 얻다, 이기다(win-won-won)

▲ 대관식 가운을 입고 있는 빅토리아 여왕의 초상화
(Henry Pierce Bone [Public domain], via Wikimedia Commons)

But in 1840, Victoria married a German prince, Albert. The prime minister found that his influence was coming to an end while Albert's influence was on the rise. Though there was no doubt that Victoria had a strong mind of her own, she depended heavily on Albert. This pattern of dependence and loyalty would continue throughout her reign as Victoria developed deep and trusting

▲ 빅토리아 여왕과 앨버트 왕자

relationships with those who would provide invaluable aid to her. The British people, however, were not always as keen on these trusted advisors, beginning with Prince Albert. It did not change the queen's mind about him. She was completely devoted to him and wholeheartedly supported his interests, which ultimately turned out very well for Britain.

- **influence** 영향(력); 영향을 주다
- **come to an end** 끝나다, 죽다(come-came-come)
- **be on the rise** 증가하고 있다
- **there is no doubt that** ~이 틀림 없다
  (*cf.* doubt 의심, 의혹)
- **have a strong mind** 의지가 강하다
- **of one's own** 스스로
- **depend heavily** 전적으로 의존하다
- **dependence** 의존, 의지
- **loyalty** 충성, 충실
- **relationship** 관계, 관련성
- **provide** 제공하다, (법률이) 규정하다
- **invaluable** 매우 유용한, 귀중한
- **aid** 도움, 지원
- **keen on** ~을 아주 좋아하는, ~에 관심이 많은
- **be devoted to** ~에 전념하다
- **wholeheartedly** 진심으로, 성실하게
- **interest** 관심, 흥미
- **ultimately** 궁극적으로, 결국
- **turn out** ~인 것으로 밝혀지다, 모습을 나타내다

In 1851, Albert's interests in art, science, and industry led him to organize the Great Exhibition, also called the Crystal Palace Exhibition for the main building in which the event was temporarily housed.  International vendors brought their products to be displayed in this world's fair, and it was quite an impressive success. Over six million people visited the site in the six months it was in London! The profits were later used to purchase lands for both industrial and cultural museums, buildings that include some of the world's most famous museums today.

▲ 1851년의 수정궁 박람회를 묘사한 그림
(By Read & Co. Engravers & Printers [Public domain],
via Wikimedia Commons)

- **industry** 산업, 공업
- **organize** 조직하다, 준비하다
- **the Great Exhibition** 대영 박람회
  (*cf.* exhibition 박람회, 전시회)
- **Crystal Palace** 수정궁(1851년 런던에 철골과
  유리로 만들어 세웠던 만국 박람회용 건물)
- **temporarily** 일시적으로, 임시로
- **house** 수용하다, 장소를 제공하다
- **vendor** 행상인, 판매 회사
- **display** 전시하다, 보여주다
- **fair** 박람회; 공정한
- **impressive** 인상적인, 훌륭한
- **profit** 이익, 수익
- **purchase** 구매하다, 사다

Aha! Culture

the Great Exhibition 대영 박람회

1851년에 영국 런던에서 열렸던 만국 박람회로, 빅토리아 여왕의 남편인 앨버트 공이 주도해 만들었어요. 박람회장이 열린 수정궁(Crystal Palace)은 정원사 출신인 조지프 팩스턴(Joseph Paxton)이 철골 구조와 유리로 만들었다고 해요. 이 박람회에 출품된 것들은 영국 본국과 식민지에서 온 것으로 10만 건이 넘었다고 하죠. 그중 가장 인기가 있었던 것은 1850년 초에 빅토리아 여왕에게 바쳐졌던 106캐럿의 커다란 인도산 다이아몬드였다고 하네요.

There's the Victoria and Albert Museum, the world's largest museum of decorative arts, covering twelve and a half acres. And the Science Museum, one of England's major tourist attractions, is

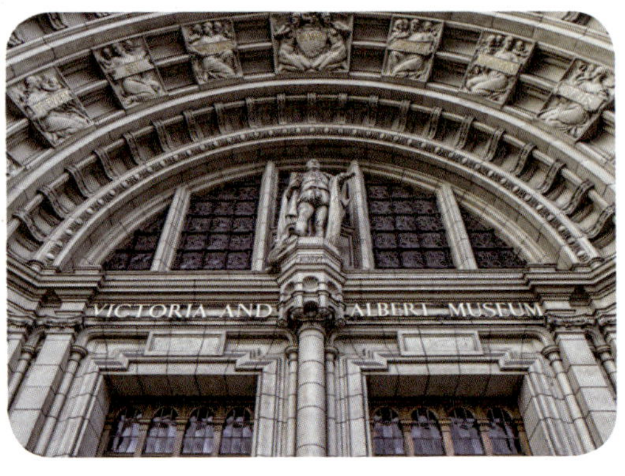

▲ Victoria and Albert Museum 빅토리아 & 앨버트 박물관

visited by thousands of British students every year. And any visitor to Exhibition Road in Kensington, home to these and other museums, would be sure to take a look inside the National Museum of History to see its towering dinosaur skeletons!

ⓔ 目路

📖 Aha! English

She was a great benefactor, providing not only her influence but funds, too.

그녀는 또한 영향력뿐만 아니라 자금도 제공하는 훌륭한 후원자였다.

'…뿐만 아니라 ~도'라는 표현은 'not only … but (also) ~'로 나타낼 수 있어요.

ex. He changed not only France but also the world. 그는 프랑스뿐만 아니라 세계도 변화시켰다.

Victoria's support went far beyond the building of museums, though. She encouraged inventors, architects and scientists. She was a great benefactor, providing not only her influence but funds, too. 📖 Many notable figures of her time, including the great naturalist, Charles Darwin, benefited from Victoria's support. 🌐

▲ Charles Darwin 찰스 다윈

- **decorative art** 장식 미술(벽걸이나 장신구처럼 사람이 거주하는 공간과 신체 주변을 장식할 목적으로 만들어지는 조형 미술)
- **acre** 에이커(약 4,050평방미터에 해당하는 크기의 땅)
- **attraction** 명소, 끌림, 매력
- **home** 본거지, 발상지, (다른 사람의 보살핌이 필요한 사람들을 위한) 시설[거주지]
- **be sure to + 동사원형** ~하기 마련이다
- **towering** 우뚝 솟은, 대단히 뛰어난
- **skeleton** 해골

- **go beyond** ~을 넘어서다(go-went-gone)
- **encourage** 격려하다, 용기를 북돋우다
- **architect** 건축가
- **benefactor** 후원자
- **not only A but (also) B** A뿐만 아니라 B도
- **fund** 자금, 기금
- **figure** 인물, 사람
- **naturalist** 동식물 연구가, 박물학자
- **benefit** (~에서) 득을 보다

🌐 Aha! Culture

Charles Darwin 찰스 다윈

빅토리아 여왕 시대 영국의 생물학자인 찰스 다윈은 '생물은 진화한다'는 이론을 적은 〈종의 기원〉으로 유명해요. 그의 이론은 당시의 창조론(모든 생물체는 하나님의 창조적 산물이라는 주장)을 믿고 있던 사회에 충격을 던졌고, 사회 전반에 큰 영향을 미쳤어요.

Sadly, Victoria's life changed drastically around this period. Her beloved husband, Albert, died of typhoid fever in December of 1861. Albert had been a powerful influence in her life as a monarch and Victoria was devastated.

Her grief was so profound that Victoria dressed in black for the next twenty-five years! But she did not, as people believed, disappear from courtly life following her husband's death. Victoria continued her royal duties despite her mourning. She kept up correspondence and granted audiences to ministers and other public officials. Even so, people were distressed at her general absence and there were complaints that she wasn't earning her income.

- **drastically** 급격히, 철저하게, 과감하게
- **period** 시기, 시대
- **beloved** 사랑하는, 인기 많은
- **die of** ~로 죽다
- **typhoid (fever)** 장티푸스
- **devastate** 엄청난 충격을 주다, 비탄에 빠지다
- **profound** 엄청난, 깊은
- **dress in black** 검은색 옷을 입다
- **disappear from** ~에서 사라져 없어지다
- **courtly** 궁정의, 우아한, 품위 있는
- **duty** 의무, 직무
- **mourning** 애도, 슬픔
- **keep up correspondence** 서신 왕래를 계속하다
- **grant** 승인하다, 허락하다, 주다
- **audience** 접견, 알현, 청중
- **public official** 공무원, 관리
- **even so** 그렇기는 하지만
- **distressed** 괴로워하는, 고민하는
- **general** 일반적인, 전면적인; 장군
- **absence** 부재, 결석
- **complaint** 불평, 불만
- **earn** (돈을) 벌다, (명성·지위 등을) 획득하다
- **income** 소득, 수입

▲ (John Jabez Edwin Mayall [Public domain], via Wikimedia Commons)

She chose the ten-year anniversary of her husband's death to make a very public appearance. Her son, the Prince of Wales, had miraculously recovered from the same disease that had killed his father, typhoid. Victoria attended a service of Thanksgiving for him at St. Paul's Cathedral in 1871. With that appearance, she began to work her way back into the hearts of her people.

▲ 존 브라운과 빅토리아 여왕
(By George Washington Wilson (1823-1893)
[Public domain], via Wikimedia Commons)

Her family, however, were not as happy with the queen. They had become increasingly concerned about a friendship between Victoria and a Scotsman and servant named John Brown. They worried about Brown's influence and her strong loyalty to him. It didn't help that sentiment in Europe was, once again, very much against the monarchy.

Aha! Culture

monarchy 군주제

정치 제도의 하나로 국가 최고 권력을 가진 군주(왕)가 그 국가의 중요한 일들을 결정하고 시행하는 거예요. 이 정치 제도는 국민이 대통령을 선거를 통해 뽑는 공화제와 대비되죠. 현재 이 제도를 유지하고 있는 나라는 영국, 네덜란드, 덴마크, 말레이시아, 태국 등이 있어요.

Benjamin Disraeli, her prime minister, stepped in with a new plan for the queen. In 1877, he decided that she should be named Empress of India. Although India had been a part of the crown since 1858, Victoria's new position strengthened that bond and her popularity exploded! John Brown died a few years later, and Victoria watched as Britain grew to become the most powerful nation in the world.

▲ Benjamin Disraeli 벤저민 디즈레일리
(By Cornelius Jabez Hughes, British
(1819 - 1884, London, England London, England)
[Public domain], via Wikimedia Commons)

▲ Queen Victoria 빅토리아 여왕
(Thomas Kennington [Public domain],
via Wikimedia Commons)

- **anniversary** 기념일, 기일
- **make an appearance** 등장하다(make-made-made)
- **miraculously** 기적적으로
- **recover** 회복하다, 되찾다
- **disease** 질병
- **attend** 참석하다, 출석하다
- **service** 예배, 의식, 봉사
- **cathedral** 대성당
- **work one's way** 노력하며 나아가다
- **increasingly** 점점 더, 갈수록 더
- **concerned about** ~을 염려하는
- **Scotsman** 스코틀랜드 사람
- **servant** 하인, 부하
- **sentiment** 정서, 감성
- **be against** ~에 반대하다
- **monarchy** 군주제, 군주국
- **step in** 돕고 나서다, 개입하다
- **empress** 여자 황제, 여제
- **strengthen** 강화하다, 강화되다
- **bond** 연대, 동맹
- **popularity** 인기
- **explode** 폭발적으로 증가하다
- **nation** 국가, 국민

Still, Victoria's nation had another side, the life that the popular author of the day, Charles Dickens, wrote about in his many novels.  Poverty was a problem during the 1800s, especially as England went from a rural economy towards the Industrial Revolution. After all, the population more than doubled in size

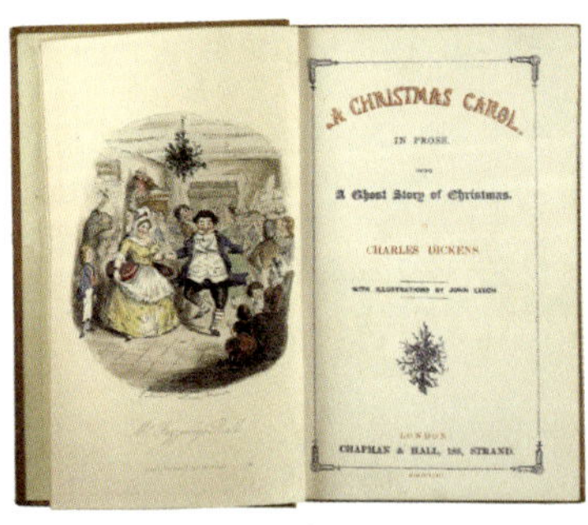

▲ 찰스 디킨스의 〈크리스마스 캐럴〉
(John Leech [Public domain],
via Wikimedia Commons)

during Victoria's reign. Many children worked as well as adults. But despite the picture painted in works such as Dickens' *A Christmas Carol*, Victoria was responsible for many reforms that eased the suffering of the poor.

- **of the day** 당시의, 오늘의
- **poverty** 빈곤, 가난
- **rural economy** 농촌 경제
- **Industrial Revolution** 산업 혁명
- **after all** 결국에는, 어쨌든
- **more than** ~ 이상의

- **double in size** 규모가 2배가 되다
- **as well as** ~뿐만 아니라
- **be responsible for** ~을 책임지고 있다, ~에 책임이 있다
- **reform** 개혁, 개선; 개혁하다
- **ease** (고통, 불편 등을) 덜어 주다
- **suffering** 고통, 괴로움(*cf.* suffer 고통받다, 시달리다)

🌐 Aha! Culture

Charles Dickens 찰스 디킨스

빅토리아 여왕 시대에 활동한 영국의 대표적인 소설가예요. 그의 작품으로는 〈크리스마스 캐럴〉, 〈위대한 유산〉, 〈올리버 트위스트〉 등이 유명해요. 그는 가난한 사람들에 대한 깊은 동정과 사회의 어두운 실제 모습들을 이야기 형식을 통해 자세히 묘사했죠. 특히, 〈크리스마스 캐럴〉에는 산업 혁명 후인 19세기 영국의 가난한 이들의 애환이 잘 나타나 있어요. 이 소설이 발표된 이후, 당시 영국의 문제가 사회적으로 논의되면서 개선되기 시작했다고 해요.

For example, consider the *Vaccination Act*, which made free vaccinations available. Or the *Railway Regulation Act*, which included a provision that would allow the poor to travel at a more affordable price. In 1863, in fact, the railways and the London Underground were built, thanks to her support.

And when the monarch used chloroform during the birth of her eighth child, the use of this powerful anesthetic became widespread. No longer would women suffer through painful and natural childbirth because, after all, Queen Victoria herself had used the drug!

- **vaccination** 예방 접종
- **act** 법률, 행동
- **available** 이용할 수 있는, 구할 수 있는
- **regulation** 규제, 단속, 규정
- **provision** (법률) 규정, 조항, 공급
- **affordable** (가격이) 알맞은, 줄 수 있는
- **London Underground** 런던 지하철
- **thanks to** ~ 덕분에
- **chloroform** (마취제의 일종) 클로로폼
- **anesthetic** 마취제
- **widespread** 널리 퍼진, 광범위한
- **no longer** 더 이상 ~아닌[하지 않는]
- **natural childbirth** 자연 분만
- **drug** 약, 마약

There were other changes, too. Because of government reforms during her reign, England avoided much of the political upheaval going on in Europe. The monarchy doubled in size, including Canada, Australia, and parts of Africa and the South Pacific as well as India. It was said that the sun never set on the British Empire, and Victoria made sure that saying remained true for a very long time.

▲ 영국 제국의 확장을 보여주는 지도
(Walter Crane [Public domain], via Wikimedia Commons)

- **government** 정부, 통치 체제
- **avoid** 피하다, 막다
- **upheaval** 대변동, 격변
- **go on** 벌어지다, 계속되다
- **the South Pacific** 남태평양
- **it is said that** ~이라고 한다
- **set** (해·달이) 지다(set-set-set)
- **empire** 제국
- **make sure (that)** ~을 확실히 하다
- **remain** 남다, 남아 있다

When, in January of 1901, the queen died, she had reigned for sixty-three years! Her funeral requests were both interesting and detailed. She asked for her beloved Albert's dressing gown as well as a plaster cast of his hand to be buried along with her. She also remembered her faithful servant, John Brown. A lock of his hair was buried with her. As for her journals—she had 122 volumes!—her daughter, Beatrice, was named as a literary executor, charged with carrying out her mother's wishes. She examined the queen's prolific writings and though she edited the queen's words, and even burned many of the pages, much of what Queen Victoria wrote survives today. Her words give the world an inside look into what it meant to be a monarch for most of the 1800s.

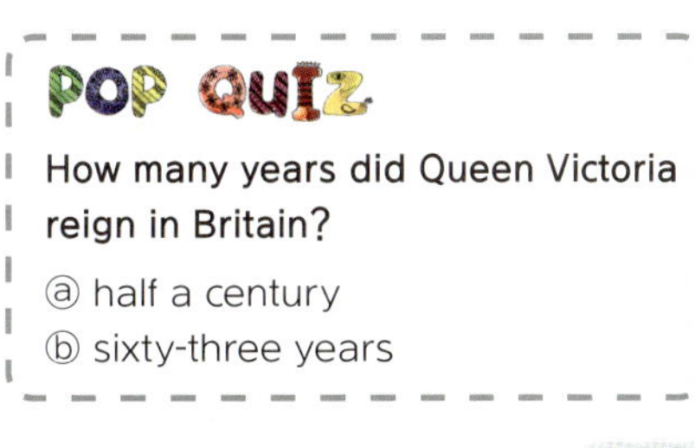

정답 ⓑ

- **request** 요구 (사항); 요청하다
- **detailed** 상세한
- **dressing gown** (잠옷 위에 입는) 가운
- **plaster cast** 깁스
- **bury** (시신을) 묻다, 매장하다
- **along with** ~와 함께
- **faithful** 충직한, 충실한
- **a lock of hair** 한 타래의 머리(*cf.* lock (함께 뭉쳐져 있거나 흘러내린 몇 올의) 머리카락)
- **volume** (시리즈로 된 책) 권
- **literary executor** 유저 관리자(사망한 저작자의 미발표 작품이나 저작물의 관리를 위탁받은 사람)
- **be charged with** ~의 책임을 지고 있다 (*cf.* charge 책임을 맡기다; 책임져야 하는 사람)
- **carry out** 수행하다, 완수하다
- **examine** 조사하다, 검토하다
- **prolific** 많은, 다작하는
- **edit** 편집하다, 수정하다

Amazingly, Victoria's influence did not end with her death. Her nine children's marriages formed important ties throughout Europe. Her grandchildren, numbered at forty-two, guaranteed a dynasty for many years to come. And so Victoria earned the title, "Grandmother of Europe."

- **tie** (강한) 유대 관계
- **throughout** 곳곳에, ~의 도처에
- **number** (합한 수가) 모두 ~이 되다, 번호를 매기다
- **guarantee** 보장하다, 약속하다
- **dynasty** 왕조, 시대
- **for many years to come** 앞으로도 오랫동안
- **title** 칭호, 직함, 제복
- **entire** 전체의, 완전한
- **presence** 존재, 참석
- **booming** 급격히 발전하는, 굉장한
- **struggle** 투쟁, 분투
- **era** 시대, 시기
- **prosperity** 번영, 번성
- **remarkably** 매우, 두드러지게
- **shaky** 불안정한, 불확실한
- **Golden Age of Empire** 제국의 전성기[황금기]
- **thriving** 번성하는, 번화한
  (*cf.* thrive 번영하다, 부자가 되다)

It's not every day that an entire period of history is named for someone. But Victoria was a towering presence among monarchs, even though she was only five feet tall. And despite the booming population and the economic struggles, the Victorian era has become known for its peace and prosperity. The queen's remarkably long reign, though shaky at the start, is remembered as the Golden Age of Empire, with the monarchy thriving and the people thriving along with the monarch!

▼ 영국의 황금기로 여겨지는 빅토리아 시대의 모습
(William Powell Frith [Public domain], via Wikimedia Commons)

Chapter One

Comprehension Quiz

A 밑줄 친 부분에 들어갈 알맞은 말에 동그라미 하세요.

❶ Victoria's support went beyond the building of (<u>museums</u> / <u>churches</u>).

❷ The queen encouraged architects and (<u>vendors / inventors</u>).

❸ Charles Darwin was a (<u>naturalist / psychologist</u>).

B 다음 내용이 옳으면 T, 틀리면 F에 표시하세요.

❶ Victoria's reign is the longest among all British monarchs. T F

❷ When Victoria died, she had a plaster cast buried with her. T F

❸ Victoria requested that strands of John's Brown hair be in her casket. T F

❹ Victoria had only a few volumes of her journals when she died. T F

❺ Many of the pages of Victoria's journals were burned. T F

Answers

A ❶ museums   ❷ inventors   ❸ naturalist

B ❶ F   ❷ T   ❸ T   ❹ F   ❺ T

 다음 질문에 알맞은 답을 고르세요.

❶ Why did people complain when Queen Victoria went into mourning?

a) They thought she neglected the royal palace.

b) They felt she ignored all of her children.

c) They thought she wasn't fulfilling her duties as Queen.

d) They believed she was stealing from the people.

❷ Why did Victoria's family worry about the Scotsman, John Brown?

a) They thought Brown had too much influence over the queen.

b) They were afraid that he would kidnap Victoria.

c) They had concerns about Brown's political background.

d) They were sure he wanted money from the queen.

❸ Despite economic struggles, what was the Victorian era known for?

a) a queen who was in mourning for life

b) peace and prosperity

c) children working long hours

d) the influence of a German prince

Answers

C ❶ c ❷ a ❸ b

Napoleon Bonaparte, Determined Military Genius

단호한 군사 천재, 나폴레옹 보나파르트

▼ (Jacques-Louis David [Public domain], via Wikimedia Commons)

Napoleon Bonaparte was a man who did not believe in giving up. "The word impossible," he famously said, "is not in my dictionary." Time and time again, this French general and political leader appeared to be down and out, only to gloriously rise again!

Napoleon was born on the island of Corsica in 1769, just a year after the small piece of Italian land came under French rule. Not surprisingly, when he attended military school on the mainland of France, he was an outsider, knowing little of his new country's customs. No one would have guessed, looking at his rank in his graduating class—he was 47th out of 58—that this student would become one of the world's greatest military leaders!

> **POP QUIZ**
>
> **Why was Napoleon Bonaparte considered an outsider in his school?**
>
> ⓐ He did not speak French.
> ⓑ He was from Corsica, which had been under Italian rule.

- **determined** 단호한, 완강한
- **believe in** ~을 옳다고 생각하다, ~의 존재를 믿다
- **give up** 포기하다(give-gave-given)
- **famously** 유명하게, 훌륭하게
- **time and time again** 몇 번이고 계속해서
- **appear** ~로 보이다, 나타나다
- **down and out** 패할 것이 분명한, 빈털터리인
- **gloriously** 훌륭히, 멋지게
- **rise again** 소생하다(rise-rose-risen)
- **come under** ~의 관할하에 들어가게 되다
- **rule** 통치, 지배, 규칙
- **not surprisingly** 놀랄 것 없이
- **military school** (육군) 사관학교
- **mainland** 본토
- **outsider** (사회·집단의 일부로 받아들여지지 않는) 국외자[아웃사이더]
- **custom** 관습, 풍습
- **rank** 지위, 등급
- **graduating class** 졸업반
- **out of** ~ 중에(서), ~의 밖으로

In the beginning of his career, however, Napoleon's heart was with his homeland. He yearned for an independent Corsica, free of French rule. And so he returned to the island, spending his time studying strategy and waiting to make his move. 📖 It was the year 1789 and the French Revolution had already brought violent changes to the mainland's government. However, Napoleon's efforts in Corsica never got off the ground. And so the young soldier, determined to make his military mark, left his island to join forces with the new government in France. And Napoleon never looked back.

- **heart** 마음, 핵심, 심장
- **yearn (for)** 갈망하다, 동경하다
- **independent** 독립된, 독립적인
- **strategy** (군사적인) 전략, 계획
- **make one's move** 행동을 일으키다
- **the French Revolution** 프랑스 혁명(1789~1799)
- **get off the ground** 순조롭게 출발하다
  (get-got-gotten)
- **be determined to + 동사원형** ~하기로 하다
- **make one's mark** 성공하다, 이름을 떨치다
  (*cf.* mark (사회적) 명성, 흔적; 특징짓다, 나타내다)
- **join forces with** ~와 협력하다
- **promote** 진급시키다, 승진시키다, 촉진하다
- **brigadier general** 준장(군대 계급 중 하나로 대령의 위, 소장의 아래를 말함)

- **put in charge of** ~의 책임을 맡다(put-put-put)
- **ups and downs** 성쇠, 오르내림
- **the Directory** (1795~1799년 프랑스 혁명 때) 집정 내각(= Directoire)
- **republic** 공화국(주권을 가진 국민이 직접 또는 간접 선거에 의하여 일정한 임기를 가진 국가 원수를 뽑는 국가 형태)
- **face** 직면하다, 마주하다; 얼굴
- **royalist** 왕정주의자[왕당파], 군주(제) 지지자
- **insurrection** 반란 사태, 봉기
- **grossly** 극도로, 지독히
- **outnumber** 수적으로 우세하다
- **repel** 물리치다, 격퇴하다
- **revolt** 반란, 봉기
- **major general** 소장

📖 Aha! English

And so he returned to the island, spending his time studying strategy ~. 그래서 그는 섬으로 돌아와 전략을 공부하면서 시간을 보내며 ~.

'~하면서 시간을 보내다'라는 표현은 'spend + 시간 + 동사원형-ing'로 나타낼 수 있어요.

ex. He spent his time watching TV. 그는 TV를 보면서 시간을 보냈다.

He rose rapidly in the ranks of the army. By the age of twenty-four, he had been promoted to brigadier general and put in charge of France's Army of Italy. Napoleon continued to thrive through the ups and downs of the new government. Now known as the Directory, the republic faced a royalist insurrection in 1795. Despite being grossly outnumbered, Napoleon and *his* forces repelled the revolt. He was only twenty-six years old, and was immediately promoted to major general!

▲ 방데미에르 13일 쿠데타[반란]

(1795년 10월 5일, 파리에서 왕당파와 혁명 정부 사이에 일어난 전투로 정부는 이것을 쿠데타라고 규정했다.)

(By Charles Monnet (Own work) [Public domain], via Wikimedia Commons)

Napoleon's lofty ambitions matched his rank. He was next
tasked with the invasion of England. Knowing that his navy
could not defeat the Royal Navy, Napoleon instead proposed
to invade Egypt so that British trade routes to India could
be cut off. He enjoyed a decisive victory at the Battle of the

Pyramids in 1798.
And then in 1799, seeing
an opportunity back in
France, Napoleon left
Egypt to take up arms
against the Directory!

▲ Battle of the Pyramids 피라미드 전투

- **lofty** 아주 높은, 고귀한
- **ambition** 야망, 의욕
- **task** (~에게) 과업을 맡기다
- **invasion** 침략, 침입
- **defeat** 물리치다, 이기다; 패배
- **the Royal Navy** 영국 해군
- **propose** 제안하다, 제시하다
- **invade** 침략하다, 침입하다
- **trade route** 통상로, 무역로
- **cut off** ~을 차단하다(cut-cut-cut)
- **decisive** 결정적인, 중대한

- **opportunity** 기회
- **take up arms against** ~에 맞서 싸울 준비를 하다
- **takeover** (권위·지배 등의) 탈취
- **director** (프랑스 혁명 정부의) 집정관, 책임자
- **coup** 쿠데타, (불의의) 일격
- **be replaced with** ~로 교체되다
- **consulate** 통령, 집정관, 영사관
- **consul** (프랑스 역사) 집정, 통령
  (1799~1804년의 최고 행정관)
- **military strategist** 군사 전략가
- **excel** 뛰어나다, 탁월하다

Aha! Culture

Battle of the Pyramids 피라미드 전투

이 전투는 1798년 7월 21일에 이집트 카이로 근교의 엠바베에서 발발한 것으로 '엠바베 전투'라고도 불려
요. 나폴레옹이 이끄는 프랑스군과 당시 이집트를 지배하던 맘루크군 사이의 전투로 나폴레옹이 여기서 승리
하게 돼요. 맘루크는 이슬람교로 개종한 노예 부대 이름으로 아랍어로는 '소유된 자'라는 뜻이라고 하네요.

▲ 제1통령인 나폴레옹의 초상화
(Jean Auguste Dominique Ingres
[Public domain or Public domain],
via Wikimedia Commons)

Napoleon joined forces for the takeover with Emmanuel Sieyès, one of the new directors, and the coup was successful.  The Directory was replaced with a three-member consulate, and Napoleon became first consul. It was during this time that he made his mark as more than a military strategist. Napoleon would excel as a strong political leader, too.

Who did Napoleon join forces with in order to stage a coup against the Directory?

ⓐ the King of England
ⓑ Emmanuel Sieyès, a director

정답 ⓑ

🌐 Aha! Culture

Emmanuel Sieyès 에마뉘엘 시에예스

프랑스 정치가로 〈제3신분이란 무엇인가〉라는 책을 발표하며 프랑스 혁명의 방향과 제3신분(시민, 농민, 노동자)의 포부를 나타냈다고 해요. 1799년에 나폴레옹의 쿠데타를 선동하는 역할을 했고, 나폴레옹이 통치하는 동안 원로원 의원이자 귀족으로 제2통령을 지냈죠.

He understood the needs of the people. Napoleon knew the people were tired of civil wars and the chaos in their country. As first consul, he was determined to restore stability to post-Revolution France.

He also embraced many of the ideals of the French Revolution, including liberty and equality. With those traits in mind, he proposed the new and much improved Constitution of the Republic. It provided for freedom of religion and an end to hereditary privilege where men would pass down their possessions and titles to their children. It had been a common practice in Europe's feudal system. Under the new Constitution, there would be equality for *all* men!

What did Napoleon wish to achieve as first consul?

ⓐ He wanted to conquer the known world.
ⓑ He wanted to restore stability in France.

ⓑ 답정

- **need** 필요, 욕구
- **be tired of** ~에 싫증이 나다
- **civil war** 내전(*cf.* civil 국내의, 시민의)
- **chaos** 혼돈, 무질서
- **restore** 회복시키다, 부활시키다, 복원하다
- **stability** 안정, 안정감
- **post-** 후의, 뒤의
- **embrace** 받아들이다, 포용하다
- **ideal** 이상, 궁극의 목적
- **liberty** 자유
- **equality** 평등
- **improved** 개선된, 향상된
- **constitution** 헌법
- **hereditary** 세습되는, 유전적인
- **privilege** 특권, 특전
- **pass down** ~을 (후대에) 물려주다
- **possession** 소유물, 소지, 보유
- **common practice** 보통 있는 일, 통례
  (*cf.* practice 관행, 관습)
- **feudal system** 봉건 체제[제도](중세 유럽에서 영주가 신하에게 땅을 주는 대신에 군역의 의무를 부과하는, 주종 관계를 기본으로 한 통치 제도)

Now, Napoleon began a different sort of campaign, bringing many reforms to France. The terrible squalor in Paris was transformed into a beautiful city, with enchanting parks and boulevards. He founded a better banking system that is still used today. But perhaps his most enduring and impressive legacy is the Napoleonic Code.

▲ Napoleonic Code 나폴레옹 법전
(DerHexer, Wikimedia Commons, CC-by-sa 4.0 [CC BY-SA 4.0
(http://creativecommons.org/licenses/by-sa/4.0) or CC BY-SA 3.0
(http://creativecommons.org/licenses/by-sa/3.0)],
via Wikimedia Commons)

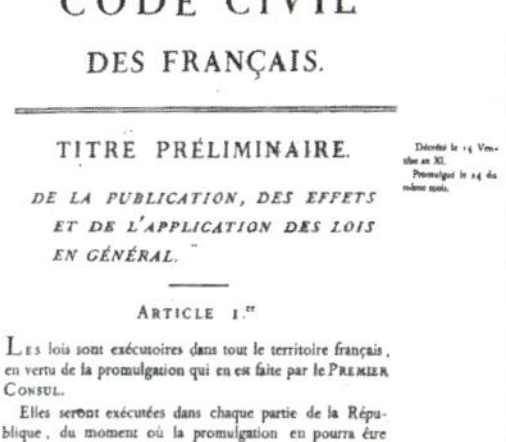

▲ 나폴레옹 법전의 초판 첫 페이지
(By Imprimerie nationale
(Scanned image on Gallica)
[Public domain],
via Wikimedia Commons)

- **a sort of** 일종의
- **campaign** 활동, 캠페인, 군사 작전
- **terrible** 끔찍한, 극심한
- **squalor** 불결한 상태
- **transform** 변형시키다, 바꾸다
- **enchanting** 황홀하게 하는, 매혹적인

- **boulevard** (가로수가 늘어진) 도로
- **found** 설립하다, 세우다
- **banking system** 은행 시스템
- **enduring** 지속되는, 오래 가는
- **legacy** 유산, 유물
- **code** (조직·국가의) 법규[규정], 법전, 부호

Aha! Culture

Napoleonic Code 나폴레옹 법전

1804년에 나폴레옹 1세가 제정하고 공포한 프랑스 민법전이에요. 근대 법전의 기초가 되는 것으로, 법 앞에서의 평등, 취업의 자유, 신앙의 자유, 사유 재산의 존중, 계약 자유의 원칙, 과실 책임주의 등을 기본으로 하고 있죠. 각 나라 민법의 근거가 되었어요. 이 법전은 함무라비 법전, 유스티니아누스 법전과 함께 세계 3대 법전중 하나로 꼽혀요.

Did Napoleon have a grand vision for his code? It's hard to say, because at the time, he simply wanted to clean up the mess that was France's legal system. There weren't really laws in the country as there were customs, and these were different from town to town. Favors and special privileges had been granted to feudal lords and kings. While these types of special privileges in other areas had been taken away, the legal system had not changed. So Napoleon and his commission worked hard to simplify the judicial system. They established a set of laws for the entire country. Prior laws had been based on a Roman code, written in Latin. Now, the laws were written in French, so that the people could understand them.

The heart of the Napoleonic Code was equality. There would be no more favoritism, and this ideal spread around the globe because Napoleon conquered so many other nations. The Napoleonic Code followed him to Italy, the Netherlands, and Belgium, all the way to Canada and Saudi Arabia. It's easy to see the democratic influence of the French civil code in these countries.

As Napoleon worked to bring equality at home, he managed to build one of the largest armies ever seen as he conquered most of Europe. His efforts were richly rewarded. Napoleon became a consul for life in 1802.

How were Napoleon's successful military efforts rewarded?

ⓐ He became a consul for life in 1802.
ⓑ He became Emperor of the World.

- **have a grand vision** 웅대한 뜻을 품다
- **clean up** 치우다, 청소하다
- **mess** 엉망인 상황[상태]
- **legal** 법률과 관련된, 합법의
- **favor** 특권, 권리, 호의
- **feudal lord** 봉건 영주
- **take away** 없애다, 제거하다
- **commission** 위원회, 수수료
- **simplify** 간소화하다, 간단하게 하다
- **judicial system** 사법체계, 재판제도
- **establish** (법률 등을) 제정하다, 확립하다, 수립하다
- **a set of** 일련의

- **prior** 앞선, 우선하는
- **be based on** ~에 기초하다
- **favoritism** 편애, 편파
- **spread** 퍼지다, 번지다 (spread-spread-spread)
- **conquer** 정복하다, 극복하다
- **all the way** 내내
- **democratic** 민주주의의
- **civil code** 민법, 민법전
- **richly** 후하게, 지극히 당연하게
- **reward** 보상하다, 보답하다
- **for life** 죽을 때까지, 평생

But his success only served to attract his enemies. These men did not approve of Napoleon's new order and they decided to assassinate him. Their plans were thwarted, but Napoleon made a decision of his own in 1804. He would crown himself Emperor of France so that other adversaries in Europe would think twice about assassinating a world leader!

▲ Coronation of Napoleon 나폴레옹의 대관식
(Jacques-Louis David [Public domain], via Wikimedia Commons)

- **serve** 도움이 되다, 근무[복무]하다, 복역하다, 봉사하다
- **attract** 끌어들이다, 마음을 끌다
- **approve** 찬성하다, 승인하다
- **new order** 새 방식, 신체제 (*cf.* order 체제, 명령, 수녀회)
- **assassinate** 암살하다
- **thwart** 좌절시키다, 방해하다
- **make a decision** 결정하다
- **adversary** 적, 상대방
- **think twice** 재고하다, 숙고하다 (think-thought-thought)

It seems odd that a man who valued the ideal of equality, who embraced the beliefs of the French Revolution, should choose to rule over all men as emperor. But Napoleon had always been an ambitious man, and besides, the people fully supported him. When his smaller army defeated two of the most powerful countries in the world—Russia and Austria—in 1805, there would be no doubts about the emperor. Napoleon had proved himself as the most brilliant military leader in Europe.

▲ 울름(Ulm) 전투에서 오스트리아군의 항복을 받고 있는 나폴레옹
(René Théodore Berthon [Public domain], via Wikimedia Commons)

- **odd** 이상한, 특이한
- **value** 중요시하다, 가치를 두다
- **rule over** ~을 지배[통치]하다
- **besides** 게다가, 그 밖에
- **prove** 입증하다, 증명하다
- **brilliant** 훌륭한, 멋진

But with all his success, Napoleon still had much he wished to achieve. Remember, he was not a man to give up easily. And so when his beloved wife, Josephine, was unable to give him an heir, he divorced her in 1810. He married Marie Louise and shortly afterwards, he had a son, also called Napoleon.

On the military front, Napoleon made the ill-fated decision to invade Russia. He took over 600,000 men into Russia in June, and though he ultimately would take Moscow, it was a long campaign. The bitterly cold winter defeated Napoleon's army. When he returned to France, he had barely 30,000 men. The allied forces of the Austrian and Prussian armies, old enemies of Napoleon, took advantage of the emperor's losses and advanced on Paris. Napoleon abdicated, giving up his throne to Louis XVIII. The once invincible emperor was exiled to the island of Elba in March of 1814. But he would not remain there long.

- **with all** ~에도 불구하고
- **achieve** 성취하다, 달성하다
- **heir** (왕위·작위의) 계승자, 후계자
- **be unable to + 동사원형** ~할 수 없다
- **divorce** 이혼하다
- **shortly afterward(s)** 얼마 지나지 않아, 곧
- **front** (전쟁에서) 전선, 앞
- **ill-fated** 불행하게 끝나는
- **bitterly** 몹시, 비통하게
- **barely** 간신히, 가까스로

- **allied** 동맹한, 연합한
- **Prussian** 프로이센의; 프로이센 사람
- **take advantage of** ~을 이용하다
- **loss** 인명 손실, 분실, 손해
- **advance** 진격하다, 나아가다
- **abdicate** 왕위에서 물러나다, 퇴위하다
- **invincible** 천하무적의, 불굴의
- **exile** 추방[유배]하다, 망명을 가게 만들다
- **Elba** 엘바 (섬)(이탈리아의 작은 섬으로 나폴레옹 1세의 첫 유배지)

Napoleon bided his time on Elba, gathering information from loyal supporters. There was unrest in France and the once emperor believed he could take back his country. In March of 1815, he planned a daring escape from the island. It had only taken a year, but Napoleon was back. He entered Paris, greeted by cheers, and the king, Louis XVIII, was forced to flee.

▲ (Charles de Steuben [Public domain], via Wikimedia Commons)

- **bide one's time** 때를 기다리다[엿보다]
- **unrest** 불안, 불만
- **take back** 되찾다
- **daring** 대담한, 위험한
- **be forced to + 동사원형** ~하도록 강요당하다
- **flee** 달아나다, 도망가다(flee-fled-fled)

It was, however, a short-lived success for the man who did not believe in the word "impossible." Though he had gathered an impressive army to his side, other European armies rallied against him. Napoleon would fight again, this time at the Battle of Waterloo. 

▲ 워털루 전투 모습(가운데 인물이 웰링턴 경)
(Jan Willem Pieneman [Public domain, Public domain or CC0], via Wikimedia Commons)

Napoleon faced his old enemy, Wellington, at this muddy field in Belgium. Both men were the same age, daring military strategists who knew that Europe lay in the balance.

- **short-lived** 오래가지 못하는
- **rally** 결집하다, 규합하다
- **muddy** 진흙투성이의, 진흙의
- **in the balance** 앞날을 알 수 없는 (불확실한) 상태에

Aha! Culture

Battle of Waterloo 워털루 전투

1815년에 벨기에 남동부의 워털루에서 나폴레옹이 이끄는 프랑스군이 웰링턴과 블뤼허가 이끄는 영국과 네덜란드, 프로이센 등의 연합군과 싸운 전투예요. 여기서 연합군에 패한 나폴레옹은 두 번째로 황제의 자리에서 내려와 세인트 헬레나로 유배를 가야 했죠. 이 전투에서의 패배로 프랑스와 유럽 국가 간의 23년에 걸친 전쟁도 끝이 났다고 해요.

Both armies fought throughout the long hours, and though it looked as if Napoleon would win the day, Wellington's men were at last joined by the Prussian army. It was too much for Napoleon's men to overcome. The French leader would leave the battlefield in defeat, exiled this time to the island of Saint Helena.

For perhaps the first time in his life, Napoleon did not attempt an escape, did not plan an attack to regain his position. It may have been the abdominal pains that plagued him for the last years of his life. Most historians believe that the former emperor died in 1821 of stomach cancer. Napoleon's indomitable spirit would not rise again, but the great military leader's legacy lives on in the democratic ideals seen around the world!

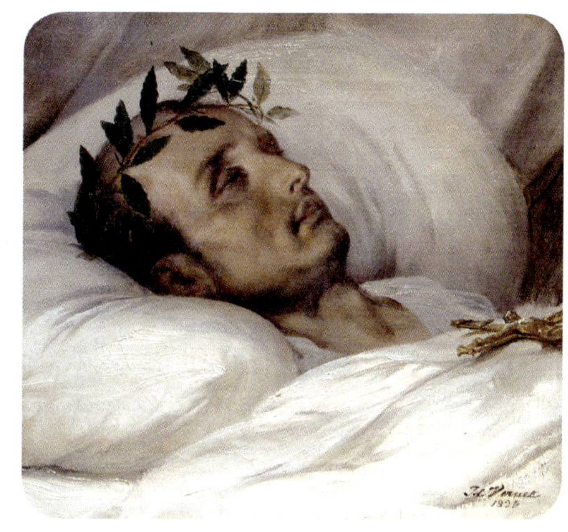

▲ 침대에 누운, 사망한 나폴레옹의 모습
(By PHGCOM [Public domain], via Wikimedia Commons)

- **win the day** 이기다, 승리하다
- **overcome** 극복하다
  (overcome-overcame-overcome)
- **battlefield** 전쟁터, 전장
- **in defeat** 패배해서
- **attempt** 시도하다
- **regain** 회복하다, 되찾다
- **abdominal pain** 복통
- **plague** 괴롭히다, 귀찮게 하다
- **former** 이전의
- **stomach cancer** 위암
- **indomitable** 불굴의, 꿋꿋한

Comprehension Quiz

A 다음 내용이 옳으면 T, 틀리면 F에 표시하세요.

❶ Napoleon ranked 47th out of 58 in his graduating class.　T　F

❷ Napoleon was put in charge of France's Army of Italy.　T　F

❸ The new government in France was known as
the Directory.　T　F

❹ Napoleon's forces were outnumbered and beaten
severely in 1795.　T　F

B 밑줄 친 부분에 들어갈 알맞은 말에 동그라미 하세요.

❶ Napoleon wanted to improve France's (legal / economic)
system.

❷ There weren't really (laws / customs) applicable throughout
France.

❸ Changes needed to be made after the (French Revolution /
Battle of the Pyramids).

❹ The new laws were written in (Latin / French), making it easier
for people.

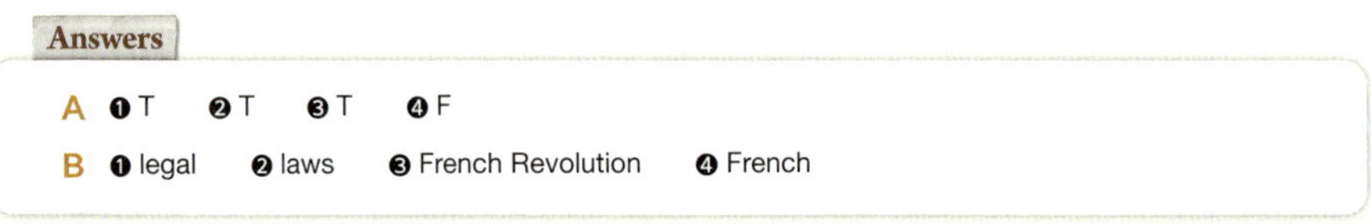

C 다음 질문에 알맞은 답을 고르세요.

❶ As first consul, which ideals of the French Revolution did Napoleon embrace?

    a) liberty and justice

    b) religious freedom and the feudal system

    c) liberty and equality

    d) freedom of speech and religion

❷ Why was Napoleon able to return to France after his first exile?

    a) The King of France was not interested in ruling the country.

    b) There was unrest in France and many people supported Napoleon.

    c) He served his term of imprisonment at Elba.

    d) The island of Elba was only a short distance from France.

❸ What is Napoleon's greatest legacy?

    a) his famous book on military strategy

    b) his democratic ideals from the Napoleonic Code

    c) the land holdings of France, won from his battles

    d) his descendants throughout the world

Chapter Three

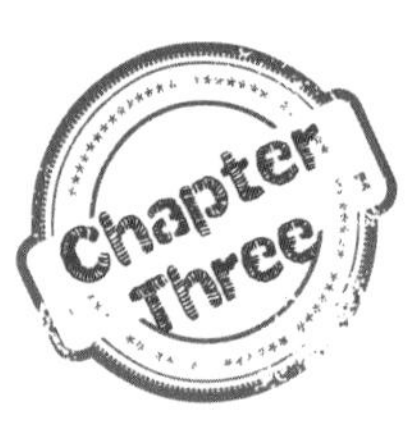

Mahatma Gandhi, Protestor for Change

변화를 위한 저항가, 마하트마 간디

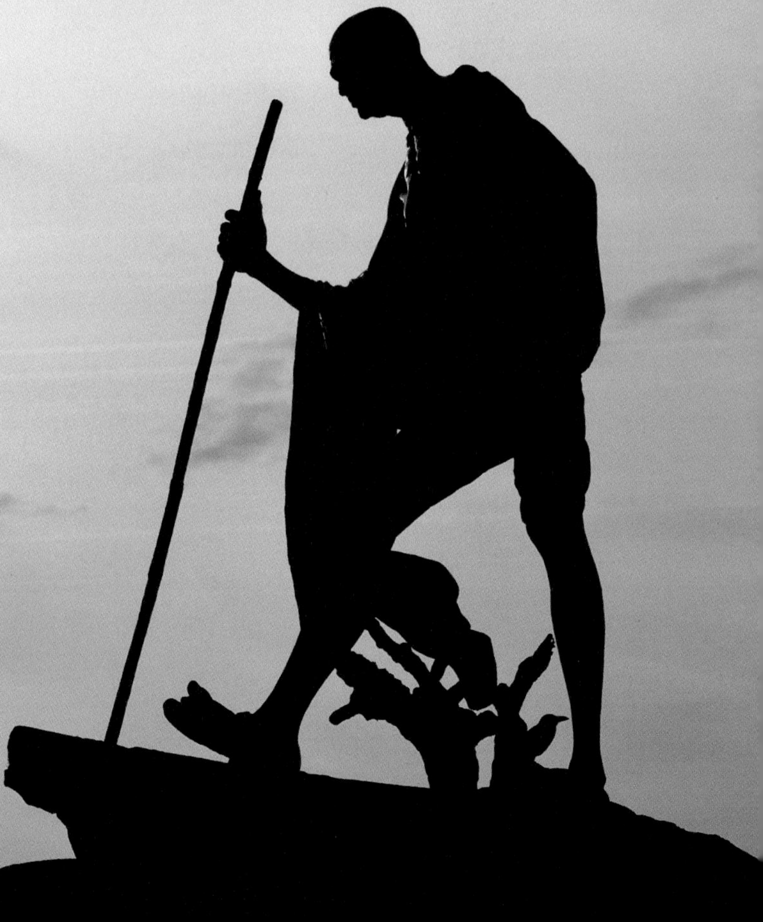

It is said that leaders are often born, not made. But Gandhi did not start out a leader. Truly, he was full of surprises from the very beginning!

The man known as a champion for the poor was born in 1869 into a well-to-do family. He was comfortably raised in the merchant class. His father held a prestigious position in the government and Gandhi was able to attend good schools where he studied English. He was 13 when he married, and even more surprising, he was a rebellious teenager, defying the Hindu beliefs of his devout mother.

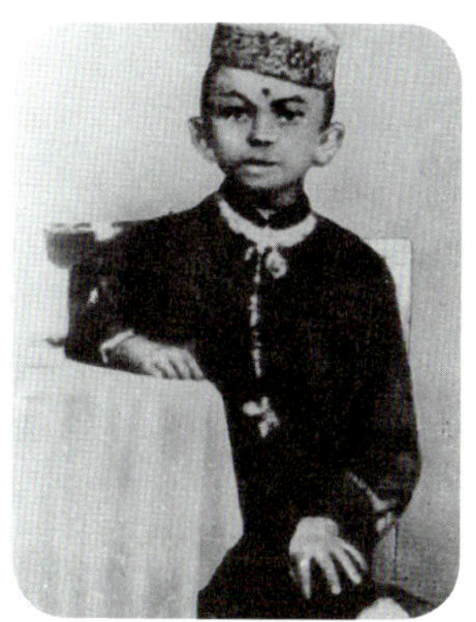

▲ 7세의 어린 간디
(See page for author [Public domain or Public domain], via Wikimedia Commons)

POP QUIZ

Which of the following is NOT true about Mahatma Gandhi?

ⓐ Gandhi's family was well-to-do.
ⓑ His mother was not very religious.

ⓑ 답정

- **start out** 시작하다
- **truly** 정말로, 진심으로
- **be full of** ~로 가득하다
- **surprise** 놀라움; 놀라게 하다
- **from the very beginning** 맨 처음부터
- **champion** 대변자, 옹호자, 챔피언
- **well-to-do** 부유한, 잘 사는
- **comfortably** 편안하게, 수월하게

- **merchant** 상인, 무역상
- **prestigious** 명망 있는, 일류의
- **be able to + 동사원형** ~할 수 있다
- **rebellious** 반항적인, 반역하는
- **defy** 거역하다, 반항하다
- **Hindu** 힌두(교)의; 힌두교 신자
- **devout** 독실한, 믿음이 깊은

How did Gandhi change his life and go on to become a larger-than-life leader for change? Several events had a transforming impact on Gandhi, but perhaps most surprising of all is that Gandhi's mission to help Indians took root in *South Africa*!

▲ 남아프리카공화국에서의 간디
(See page for author [Public domain or Public domain], via Wikimedia Commons)

Gandhi studied to be a barrister in London and then returned to India, but in Bombay, he was not a very successful lawyer. He jumped at the opportunity to go to South Africa in 1893, but he was not prepared for the prejudice that met him there.

- **go on to + 동사원형** 계속해서 ~을 하다
- **larger-than-life** 영웅적인, 전설적인, 실물보다 큰
- **have an impact on** ~에 영향을 주다
- **transforming** 변형적인
- **mission** (일생의) 사명, 임무, 포교단
- **take root** 뿌리를 내리다
- **barrister** (영국의 상위 법원에서 변론할 수 있는) 법정 변호사
- **Bombay** 봄베이(인도의 항구 도시 뭄바이(Mumbai)의 옛 이름)
- **jump at** (기회·제의 등을) 덥석 붙잡다
- **prejudice** 편견, 피해
- **turban** 터번(이슬람교도나 시크교도 남자들이 머리에 쓰는 두건)
- **magistrate** 치안 판사
- **remove** (옷 등을) 벗다, 제거하다
- **headdress** 머리에 쓰는 것, 머리 장식
- **courtroom** 법정
- **throw off** (…에게 ~을) 떠나라고 명령하다, ~을 높은 곳에서 거칠게 밀다, (옷을) 벗어 던지다 (throw-threw-thrown)
- **make up one's mind** 결심하다
- **injustice** 불평등, 부당함
- **witness** 목격하다, 증명하다

Although he dressed in a western style suit, Gandhi also wore a turban. When a magistrate asked him to remove his headdress, Gandhi refused and left the courtroom. And later, even though he was well dressed and had a first class ticket, he was thrown off a train because of his darker skin color.  Forced to spend a bitterly cold night in the station, Gandhi's views were forever changed. He made up his mind to stay in South Africa, and he would fight the injustices he'd witnessed.

📖 Aha! English

And later, even though he was well dressed and had a first class ticket, ~. 그리고 후에, 그가 제대로 갖춰 입고 일등석 표를 가지고 있었음에도 불구하고, ~.

even though는 '~에도 불구하고, 비록 ~일지라도'라는 뜻으로 가정이 아니라 실제 일어난 상황에 대해 이야기할 때 쓰는 접속사예요. 반면에 even if는 아직 일어나지 않은 일에 대해 가정해서 말해보는 표현으로 구분해서 알아두세요.

ex. Even though I'm your sister, I can't support you on this. 난 너의 언니지만, 이것에 대해서는 네 편을 들어줄 수 없다.

The young lawyer wanted to put an end to the discriminatory practices against Indian immigrants. Just a few months after the train incident, Gandhi set up the Natal Indian Congress. Meanwhile, the seeds of war were spreading in South Africa. With the Boer War in 1899, Gandhi saw an opportunity for the Indians to gain legitimacy. If they would serve in the war, he believed, then surely they would gain their citizenship rights. He organized the Indian Ambulance Corps, with 300 free Indians and 800 indentured, or contracted laborers. This was one of the few medical units set up to help wounded black South Africans, and Gandhi served as a stretcher-bearer.

- **put an end to** (악습 따위를) 없애다, 폐지하다
- **discriminatory** 차별적인, 불공평한
- **immigrant** 이민자
- **incident** 사건, (불쾌한) 일
- **set up** 건립하다, 준비하다
- **Natal** 나탈(남아프리카공화국 동부, 인도양 연안의 주)
- **congress** (여러 단체의 대표들이 모이는) 회의, 의회, 국회
- **meanwhile** 그동안에
- **seed** 씨, 근원
- **Boer War** 보어 전쟁
- **gain** 얻게 되다, 얻다
- **legitimacy** 정당성, 합법성, 타당성
- **citizenship** 시민권, 시민의 자격
- **right** 권리; 옳은
- **ambulance corps** 야전 의무대
- **indenture** 고용을 계약서로 결정하다, 도제살이로 고용하다
- **contracted** 계약된
- **laborer** 노동자
- **unit** (군사) 부대, 구성 단위
- **wounded** 부상당한, 상처 입은
- **stretcher-bearer** 들것 운반부

Aha! Culture

Natal Indian Congress / Boer War 나탈 인도인 회의 / 보어 전쟁

나탈 인도인 회의는 남아프리카공화국에 있는 인도인들이 겪고 있는 차별에 저항하기 위한 목적으로 1894년에 간디가 조직했어요. 이것은 후에 만델라가 이끌었던 아프리카 민족 회의에 큰 영향을 주었어요. 1899년에서 1902년까지 계속되었던 보어 전쟁은 아프리카에서 종단 정책을 추진하던 영국 제국과 당시 남아프리카 지역에 살던 네덜란드계 보어족 사이에서 일어난 전쟁이에요.

▲ 나탈 인도인 회의 설립자들(윗줄 왼쪽에서 4번째가 간디)
(See page for author [Public domain or Public domain], via Wikimedia Commons)

▲ 보어 전쟁 당시 인도인 야전 의무대의 들것 운반부들(중간줄 왼쪽에서 5번째가 간디)
(See page for author [Public domain], via Wikimedia Commons)

Mahatma Gandhi, Protestor for Change • **57**

But when the war ended, the Indian situation had not improved. In fact, Indians were treated even worse. In 1906, the Transvaal government required all Indians to register.  Gandhi's use of non-violent protest began when he refused to carry an identification card. Indians followed his example, employing peaceful resistance in defying the law. It was not long before they began to pay the price for this passive resistance. Indians were flogged, shot, and imprisoned. Gandhi was arrested, too, and it was in jail, in 1908, that he read Henry David Thoreau's *Civil Disobedience*. Thoreau's words inspired Gandhi even more in his fight for civil justice through non-violent protest.

- **treat** 다루다, 취급하다
- **Transvaal** 트란스발(남아프리카공화국 북동부의 주)
- **require** 요구하다, 필요로 하다
- **register** (출생·혼인·사망 사실을) 신고하다, 등록하다
- **non-violent protest** 비폭력 시위
- **identification card** 신분 증명서
- **employ** 쓰다, 이용하다, 고용하다
- **resistance** 저항, 항거
- **it is not long before** 이윽고, 잠시 후에
- **pay the price for** ~의 대가를 지급하다[치르다]

- **passive resistance** 소극적 저항 (정부나 적에 대해 명령 불복종 등과 같은 평화적인 방법으로 하는 저항)
- **flog** 태형을 내리다, 매로 때리다
- **imprison** 투옥하다, 감금하다
- **arrest** 체포하다; 체포
- **jail** 감옥, 교도소
- **disobedience** 불복종, 반항
- **inspire** 영감을 주다, 격려하다
- **justice** 정의, 정당성

Aha! Culture

Transvaal Asiatic Registration Act 트란스발 아시아인 등록법

1906년에 남아프리카공화국의 트란스발 정부가 인도인 이민 제한을 위해 부과한 지문 등록법이에요. 8년 이상 거주한 모든 인도인은 관청에 가서 이름과 주소, 카스트(계급), 나이, 직업을 신고하고 손가락 열 개 모두의 지문을 찍은 후에 등록증을 받아야 했대요. 밖에 나갈 때 모든 인도인은 이 등록증을 가지고 다녀야 했죠.

Next, Gandhi called for a strike to protest against a tax inflicted upon working class Indians, primarily the miners and the farm laborers. In 1913, he led over 2,000 people from Natal to the Transvaal, and though he was arrested and served nine months in prison, Gandhi's efforts were rewarded. The British government dropped the tax and Gandhi was released. Perhaps more importantly, Gandhi's methods of civil disobedience and passive resistance made a mark not just in South Africa but England and India, too. It was time for Gandhi to go home.

▲ 간디의 지도로 투쟁 중인 인도 광부들
(See page for author [Public domain or Public domain],
via Wikimedia Commons)

- **call for** ~을 요구하다
- **strike** 파업, (군사적) 공격
- **protest against** ~에 대해서 항의하다
- **tax** 세금
- **inflict upon** …에게 (~을) 가하다

- **primarily** 주로, 처음에는
- **miner** 광부
- **release** 석방하다, 풀어주다
- **method** 수단, 방법
- **it is time to + 동사원형** ~할 때이다

🌐 Aha! Culture

Henry David Thoreau 헨리 데이비드 소로

미국의 사상가이자 문학자인 헨리 데이비드 소로는 사회 문제에 민감하게 반응했어요. 1846년 7월, 그는 멕시코 전쟁에 반대해서 인두세(일정 연령 이상의 주민에게 부과되는 일률적인 세금) 납부를 거부한 죄로 투옥되었고, 이때의 경험을 토대로 〈시민 불복종〉을 썼죠. 이 책은 후에 간디의 시민운동에 큰 영향을 주었어요.

Gandhi returned to India after more than twenty years away, and he was not happy with the poverty in his homeland. By 1920, he was convinced that Indian independence was the only way to save his country and improve the lives of its people. He began

▲ (See page for author
[Public domain or Public domain],
via Wikimedia Commons)

his campaign for improvement with changes in the Indian National Congress (INC), a major political party. But first, Gandhi made a personal change.

He began to wear the Indian dhoti, a garment worn by Hindu males that is tied at the waist. Gandhi called the traditional white robe that replaced his suit his "mourning robe." It was his statement of solidarity, or unity, with the poor in India. He never wore anything else.

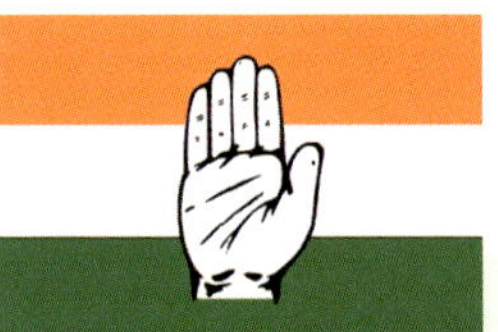

인도 국민 회의 깃발 ▶
(By Own work (Image drawn by me, Nichalp using Inkscape.)
[Public domain], via Wikimedia Commons)

🌐 Aha! Culture

Indian National Congress 인도 국민 회의(파)

1885년에 설립된 인도의 보수정당으로 현재는 보통 회의당(Congress Party)이라고 불려요. 이 단체의 설립 목적은 영국의 인도 통치를 개선하기 위함이었어요. 하지만 1905년에 영국이 행정 편의를 구실로 벵골 주를 이슬람교도 거주 지역과 힌두교도 거주 지역으로 나누어 민족의 통합을 분열시키려 하자 이에 반기를 들고 인도의 근대화 민족운동을 전개하는 방향으로 바뀌어 나갔죠.

Gandhi worked tirelessly to change the INC. Before, it had been a political party for the elite in India, those who were wealthy and of a high caste, or social class. 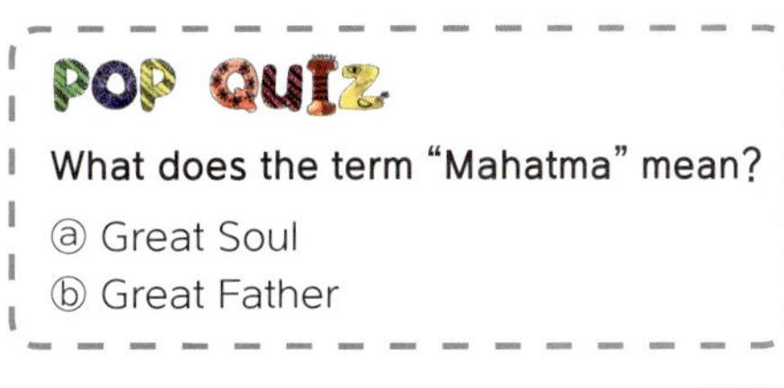 Gandhi brought the INC to *all* the people. No matter the religious faith or class, they would all embrace the idea of the non-violent, non-cooperative protest. And more than anything else, Gandhi wanted India's independence from Britain.

It was during this time that Gandhi would be called by a new name: "Mahatma," a title that means "Great Soul." Others have earned the same title, but none so famous as Mahatma Gandhi!

ⓔ 릅Ꭷ

- **convinced** 확신하는, 신념이 있는
- **independence** (국가의) 독립
- **improvement** 향상, 개선
- **party** 정당, 단체, 파티
- **dhoti** 도티(인도에서 남자들이 몸에 두르는 천)
- **garment** 의복, 옷
- **robe** 예복

- **statement** 성명(서), 표현, 진술
- **solidarity** 연대, 결속
- **unity** 통합, 통일
- **tirelessly** 지칠 줄 모르고, 끊임없이
- **caste** (힌두교 사회의) 카스트[계급]
- **non-cooperative** 비협력적인
- **soul** 영혼, 정신

Aha! Culture

인도의 신분제도

인도에는 태어날 때부터 사회적 계급이 정해져 있는데요, 이것을 '카스트(caste)'라고 불러요. 카스트 제도에서 최상위층은 '브라만(Brahmin)'으로 성직자, 학자 등이 여기에 속하고, 그다음은 '크샤트리아(Kshatriya)'로 귀족, 무사 등 국가를 통치하는 사람들이죠. 그다음 중간 계층은 '바이샤(Vaisya)'로 농민, 상인, 수공업자들이에요. 그 아래 '수드라(Shudra)'는 하인이나 노예에 해당하는 사람들을 말해요.

Unfortunately, it was Gandhi's widespread fame and success that earned him another arrest. Because his resistance movement flourished, the British government put Gandhi in jail for two years. When he was released, Indians still labored under British rule. And so Gandhi protested again.

The British Salt Laws prohibited Indians from selling or collecting salt, and worse, they had to pay an exorbitant tax for British salt. Gandhi led thousands of poor Indians on his Salt March where they boiled up salt from the water. This act was illegal, but the British were unable to control the vast numbers of protesters as well as their various acts of civil disobedience. The British gave in, and Gandhi traveled to London to represent the Indian National Congress at official talks.

▲ 소금 행진을 하는 간디와 인도인들
(By Yann (Scanned by Yann (talk).) [Public domain or Public domain], via Wikimedia Commons)

In the end, he failed to gain what he had strived so long for: Indian independence. Gandhi returned to India and vowed to quit politics. But then came World War II. Winston Churchill called for India to support the British in the war, but Gandhi did not think Indians should fight for Britain when they were still under British rule. Thus his next protest called for Britain to "Quit India" for good. 

Churchill refused to back down, and Gandhi and his wife were imprisoned. This time, the protests turned violent, erupting throughout the country! In 1944, he was finally released, but sadly, his wife died months before, while still in prison.

> ## POP QUIZ
>
> **What famous British person caused Gandhi to begin the "Quit India" campaign?**
>
> ⓐ King George VI
> ⓑ Winston Churchill

정답 ⓑ

- **flourish** 번창하다, 번성하다
- **labor** 고생하다, 일하다
- **prohibit from** ~을 금지하다
- **exorbitant** 과도한, 지나친
- **boil up** ~을 끓이다
- **illegal** 불법적인(↔ legal 법적인)

- **vast** 어마어마한, 막대한
- **give in** (~에게) 항복하다
- **represent** 대표하다, 대신하다
- **talks** 회담, 협상
- **strive** 분투하다, 애쓰다
- **vow** 서약하다, 맹세하다; 맹세

- **quit** 그만두다, 떠나다
- **thus** 따라서, 이리하여
- **for good** 영원히
- **back down** (주장 등을) 굽히다, 패배를 인정하다
- **erupt** 분출하다, 터뜨리다

🌐 Aha! Culture

Quit India Movement 인도 철수 운동

제2차 세계대전이 시작되자 영국은 인도에게 전쟁에 협력할 것을 지시해요. 하지만 간디는 협력할 수 없다고 선언하는데, 이것이 인도의 독립운동이라고 할 수 있는 '인도 철수 운동'의 시작이에요. 간디는 연설을 통해 영국에게 '인도를 떠나라!(Quit India!)'라고 말하면서 인도 철수 운동을 주도하게 돼요. 인도인들에게 '불복종 운동을 전개하라. 아니면 죽는다'라고 역설하기도 했죠.

Gandhi finally achieved independence for India, but it was not

the independence he'd envisioned. Two countries were created from one. The nations of India and Pakistan were divided along religious lines, and tragically this led

to chaos, violence, and mass killings!  War broke out between the two nations. Gandhi left for Calcutta, hoping that through his fasting, he could bring about a new peace. But on his way to a prayer meeting, he was shot three times in the chest.

- **envision** 마음속에 그리다, 상상하다
- **divide** 분리하다, 나누다
- **line** 구분, 경계, 선
- **tragically** 비극적으로, 비참하게
- **mass killing** 대량 살상(*cf.* mass 대량의)
- **break out** 발발하다(break-broke-broken)
- **Calcutta** 캘커타(인도 북동부에 있는 인도 최대 항구 도시)
- **fasting** 단식, 금식
- **bring about** 일으키다, 초래하다
  (bring-brought-brought)
- **prayer meeting** 기도회
- **nominate** (후보자로) 지명하다, 임명하다

- **discussion** 논의, 심의, 상의
- **likely** ~할 공산이 있는, ~할 것 같은
- **proponent** 지지자, 옹호자
- **weigh against** ~에 불리하게 조작하다
- **nomination** 지명, 추천
- **short list** 선발 후보자 명단
- **according to** ~에 따르면
- **committee** 위원회
- **suitable** 적합한, 적절한
- **candidate** 후보자
- **embody** (사상 등을) 구현하다, 담다
- **quote** 인용구, 인용문

🌐 Aha! Culture

인도와 파키스탄

1947년에 영국으로부터 독립하는 과정에서 인도 반도는 힌두교와 이슬람교 간의 대립으로 인해 인도와 파키스탄이라는 두 개의 나라로 분리돼요. 인도와 파키스탄은 분리 당시에 북서부의 카슈미르 지역을 놓고 전쟁을 벌였죠. 당시 카슈미르 지역은 힌두교 정권이 지배하고 있었지만 주민의 다수는 이슬람교도였어요. 이 전쟁은 유엔의 중재로 휴전되었어요.

Perhaps the biggest surprise of all in the life of Mahatma
Gandhi was that he never won the Nobel Peace Prize. He was
nominated in 1937, '38, '39, '47, and finally, in 1948. There has
been much discussion about why Gandhi never received the
award. All these years later, it seems most likely that though
Gandhi was a strong proponent of non-violence, his protests
sometimes led to violence. Sadly, this fact may have weighed
against him in the first four nominations. But in 1948, it's clear
that Gandhi *would* have won at last. First, because there were
only three names on the short list, including, of course, Gandhi.

And secondly, because according to a
statement released by the committee, the
Nobel Prize was not awarded that year as
there was "no suitable *living* candidate."
Gandhi had been assassinated on January
30th, 1948. He didn't need to receive any
awards. He lived long enough to bring
about the changes that would forever
change India. He was a leader who truly
embodied the quote he's most famous for:
You must be the change you wish to see
in the world!

▲ (See page for author
[Public domain, CC BY-SA 2.0
(http://creativecommons.org/
licenses/by-sa/2.0) or Public
domain], via Wikimedia Commons)

Comprehension Quiz

A 이야기 전개에 맞게 다음 문장들을 다시 배열하세요.

❶ Gandhi set up the Indian Ambulance Corps.

❷ Gandhi was kicked off a train because of his skin color.

❸ Gandhi encouraged immigrants to serve in the Boer War.

❹ Gandhi set up the Natal Indian Congress.

______ → ______ → ______ → ______

B 다음 내용이 옳으면 T, 틀리면 F에 표시하세요.

❶ After the Boer War, the Indian immigrants' situation greatly improved. T F

❷ The Transvaal government required all Indians to register. T F

❸ Gandhi carried an identification card in his wallet. T F

❹ Indians would pay a high price for peaceful resistance. T F

❺ The INC had been a party for the elite in India. T F

Answers

A ❷ → ❹ → ❸ → ❶
B ❶ F ❷ T ❸ F ❹ T ❺ T

 다음 질문에 알맞은 답을 고르세요.

❶ Which of the following incidents of prejudice affected Gandhi?

a) A magistrate asked him to remove his turban while in court.

b) He was called names by other lawyers in the courts.

c) He was asked to leave a plane because of his skin color.

d) He was not allowed to ride on public transportation.

❷ How did Gandhi feel about his homeland when he returned in 1920?

a) He was impressed with the level of trade success he saw.

b) He could relax because the country was on track.

c) He thought only Indian independence could save his country.

d) He was relieved that poverty had lessened a great deal.

❸ What happened when Gandhi was imprisoned from 1942~1944?

a) Protests turned violent.

b) Gandhi's wife refused to go to jail with him.

c) The British backed down and granted India independence.

d) Gandhi refused to eat and nearly died.

Answers

C ❶ a ❷ c ❸ a

Nelson Mandela, Imprisoned Freedom Fighter

수감된 자유의 전사, 넬슨 만델라

Another great leader came out of South Africa. He left the freedom of his small village only to end up spending years imprisoned so that others could be free. His name was Rolihlahla, though the world knows him better as Nelson.

- **freedom fighter** 자유의 전사(반정부 무장 투쟁을 하는 사람을 그 지지자들이 칭하는 이름)
- **principal** 중요한, 주요한; 교장
- **counselor** 고문, 상담사, 변호사
- **acting** 대행의, 대리의
- **Thembu** (남아프리카 부족) 템부족의 구성원 (*cf.* 복수형은 Thembus)
- **Christian** 기독교의; 기독교인
- **as is** (어떤 조건·상태이든) 있는 그대로
- **adopt** 입양하다, 채택하다
- **high-ranking member** 고위 인사
- **youngster** 청소년, 아이
- **inequality** 불평등
- **demonstrate** (행동으로) 보여주다, 입증하다

Nelson Mandela was born in 1918 in South Africa, the son of the principal counselor to the acting king of the Thembu people. He was sent to a Christian school and there, as was the custom, he was given the Christian name of Nelson. When he was only nine, though, his father died, and Nelson was adopted by a high-ranking member of the Thembus who had plans for the youngster. He wanted Nelson to be a great leader. And the more Nelson learned about the inequalities in his country, the more he was determined to be a leader who would bring great changes to his people. 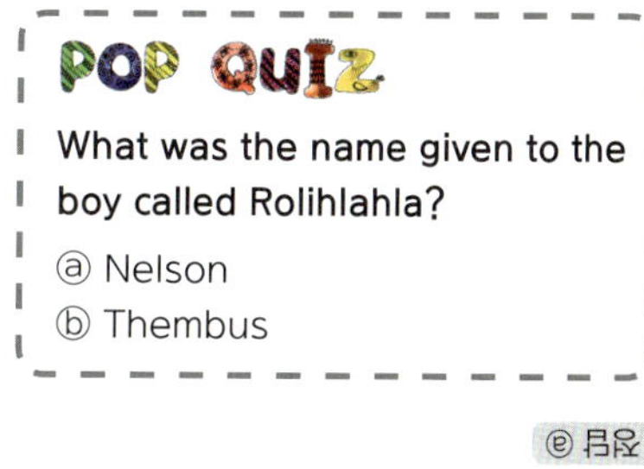 Even as a young man, Nelson Mandela would demonstrate the spirit of protest that marked his long life.

ⓔ 吕&

Aha! English

And the more Nelson learned about the inequalities in his country, the more he was determined to be a leader ~. 그리고 넬슨은 자기 나라에서의 불평등에 대해 더 많이 알아 갈수록, ~ 지도자가 되어야겠다고 더 결심을 굳혔다.

'…할수록 더 ~하다'를 영어로 말할 때는 'the + 비교급, the + 비교급' 구문을 사용할 수 있어요.

ex. The more popular his song is, the more money he makes. 그의 노래가 인기가 더 많아질수록, 그는 더 많은 돈을 번다.

▲ (See page for author
[Public domain or Public domain],
via Wikimedia Commons)

After he finished at Healdtown, a Methodist college, he attended University of Fort Hare, which was the only black institution for higher learning at that time in South Africa. But he was expelled for protesting over university policies. After being kicked out, he returned home in disgrace, where his guardian decided to arrange a marriage for him. But Nelson Mandela wanted to choose his own wife, and so he fled to Johannesburg. Still, he had more on his mind than finding a wife. He studied law through a correspondence course. He met many people who later became key figures in the fight against discrimination. And he joined the African National Congress (ANC). There, he managed the newly formed Youth League. And then, in 1948, the National Party came into power.

- **Methodist** 감리교(도)의; 감리교 신자
- **institution** 기관, 단체
- **expel** 퇴학시키다, 쫓아내다
- **policy** 정책, 방침
- **kick out** ~을 쫓아내다
- **in disgrace** 불명예스럽게
- **guardian** 후견인, 수호자
- **arrange a marriage** 혼담을 성사시키다
- **correspondence course** 통신 강좌[교육 과정]
  (방송이나 우편 따위를 통하여 하는 교육 강좌)

- **key figure** 주요 인물
- **discrimination** 차별, 구별
- **African National Congress** 아프리카 민족 회의
  (남아프리카공화국의 민족 운동 조직)
- **Youth League** 청년 동맹[연맹]
- **National Party** (남아프리카공화국) 국민당
- **come into power** 권력을 장악하다

Nelson Mandela was thirty years old when the National Party introduced the policy of apartheid in South Africa. 

▲ 흑인 출입 금지를 알리는 표지판
(By Dewet [Public domain], via Wikimedia Commons)

It's not a very big word, but it had a huge effect on black South Africans. The system of apartheid promoted segregation, the enforced separation of people by race. It also permitted discrimination based on skin color. So if you were a black South African, your rights were severely limited.

POP QUIZ

What policy permitted segregation and discrimination in South Africa?

ⓐ apartheid
ⓑ democracy

ⓔ 답정

- **introduce** 시작[도입]하다, 소개하다
- **apartheid** 아파르트헤이트
  (남아프리카공화국의 인종 차별 정책)
- **segregation** 차별 정책
- **enforced** 강제적인
- **separation** 분리, 구분
- **race** 인종, 경주
- **permit** 허용하다, 허락하다
- **severely** 심각하게, 혹독하게

🌐 Aha! Culture

apartheid 아파르트헤이트

원래 '분리·격리'를 뜻하는 아파르트헤이트는 남아프리카공화국의 인종 차별 정책으로, 백인 우월주의에 입각한 정책이에요. 1948년 국민당 정부 수립 이후, 국민의 약 16퍼센트 밖에 되지 않던 백인이 법률로 흑인과 토착민들을 정치·경제·사회적으로 차별하는 제도였어요. 이 정책에 따르면, 흑인과 토착민에 대해서는 직업을 제한하고, 도시 외곽 지역 토지 소유가 금지되었으며, 백인과의 결혼도 금지되었어요. 또한, 백인과 흑인은 같은 버스도 타지 못했죠. 이 정책은 넬슨 만델라가 1994년에 대통령이 되면서 완전 철폐됐어요.

It wasn't long before Mandela and the African National Congress took action in the form of mass civil disobedience. In the campaign for the Defiance of Unjust Laws, Mandela and others traveled across the country. They encouraged protests and attempted to overwhelm the justice system. Nelson Mandela became well known during this time, so it was not surprising when he was arrested on charges of high treason. For five years, the trial continued, and often, Mandela would sleep in jail at night and be allowed to work at his law firm during the day. Eventually, he and the others were acquitted and Mandela was finally free. But Sharpeville was coming.

Sharpeville is just a small township in Transvaal, but in 1960, it was the scene of a massacre that would shock the entire world. Sixty-nine anti-apartheid demonstrators were killed as they protested outside the Sharpeville police station. As chaos and riots swept the country, the government banned the ANC. The time for peaceful protest was over, thought Mandela and his friends. That was the beginning of the development of the military faction of the ANC called "Spear of the Nation."

▲ 샤프빌 학살 때 사망한 69명의 묘
(By Andrew Hall (Own work) [CC BY-SA 4.0
(http://creativecommons.org/licenses/by-sa/4.0)],
via Wikimedia Commons)

- **take action** 행동에 옮기다, ~에 대해 조치를 하다
- **in the form of** ~의 형식[모양]으로
- **Defiance of Unjust Laws** 부당한 법에 대한 저항
- **overwhelm** 제압하다, 압도하다
- **justice system** 사법 제도
- **on charges of** ~의 죄로, ~의 혐의로
- **high treason** 반역죄, 대역죄
- **trial** 재판, 시험
- **law firm** (대규모) 법률 사무소

- **be acquitted** 무혐의로 풀려나다
- **township** (과거 남아프리카공화국의) 흑인 거주구
- **massacre** 대학살; 대학살하다
- **demonstrator** 시위자, 시위 참가자
- **riot** 폭동, 소동
- **sweep** 휩쓸고 가다(sweep-swept-swept)
- **faction** 파벌, 파당
- **Spear of the Nation** 국민의 창(ANC의 무장 세력)

▲ 만델라가 숨어있던 초가집
(By Colinvlr (Own work) [Public domain],
via Wikimedia Commons)

It was also the beginning of Mandela going underground. He kept a low profile and stayed in hiding. But at the same time, Spear of the Nation tried to bring the government, in Mandela's words, "to its senses." They blew up railroad lines as well as government buildings. Though they had no policy to take lives, there were accidental deaths. Years later, Mandela would explain the reason behind Spear of the Nation: "It was only when all else had failed, when all channels of peaceful protest had been barred to us, that the decision was made to embark on violent forms of political struggle."

- **go underground** 지하에 숨다
- **keep a low profile** 세간의 이목을 피하다, 두드러지지 않다
- **senses** 제정신, 본정신
- **blow up** 폭발하다, 터트리다(blow-blew-blown)
- **take life** 죽이다, 목숨을 빼앗다
- **accidental** 우연한, 돌발적인
- **behind** ~ 뒤에, 이면에서
- **bar** 막다, 차단하다; 창살, 막대기
- **embark on** ~에 나서다[착수하다]

- **capture** 붙잡다, 생포하다
- **sentence** 선고하다, 판결을 내리다
- **be behind bars** 투옥되다
- **senior** (계급·지위가) 고위의
- **suburb** 교외, 시외
- **be implicated** 연루되다
- **sabotage** 사보타주(적이 사용하는 것을 막기 위해 장비, 운송 시설 등을 고의로 파괴하는 행위)
- **conspiracy** 모의, 음모

Mandela was captured in 1962 and imprisoned for leaving the country illegally. At that time, he was sentenced to serve five years. While he was behind bars, though, many of the senior members of the ANC were captured in Rivonia, a suburb of Johannesburg. Mandela was implicated along with the other men, and at the Rivonia Trial, he and the others were sentenced for treason, sabotage, and violent conspiracy. Nelson Mandela would spend the next 27 years imprisoned on Robben Island.

▲ 만델라가 있던 로벤 섬 교도소

◀ 만델라의 감방
(By Witstinkhout (Own work) [CC BY-SA 3.0
(http://creativecommons.org/licenses/by-sa/3.0)],
via Wikimedia Commons)

> ## POP QUIZ
> For how many years was Mandela imprisoned on Robben Island?
> ⓐ twenty-seven years
> ⓑ thirty-seven years

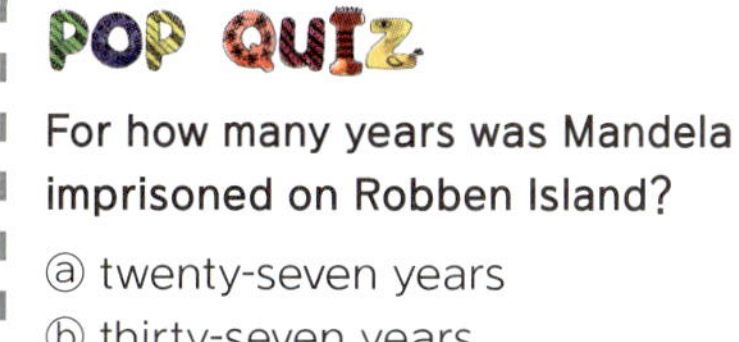

He lived in a tiny cell, alone, often stuck in solitary confinement, with no bathroom and no proper bed. He worked in the quarry, too, breaking rocks from sunrise till sundown. The government wanted to break Mandela, to humiliate him so that his followers would scatter. But Mandela continued to protest from the inside of his jail cell. Then, the international community began to gather support for him on the outside.

In 1964, for example, South Africa was banned from the Olympics and economic sanctions were upheld, too. In the 70's, Mandela smuggled out many political statements as well as his autobiography, *Long Walk to Freedom*. Though it was not published for the rest of the world until 1995, many people in South Africa would read his words. And yet, these same people did not know what Nelson Mandela, the man known for anti-apartheid in South Africa, looked like. It was against the law to print photos of him!

- **cell** 감방, 세포
- **stick in** 집 안에 있다(stick-stuck-stuck)
- **solitary confinement** 독방 감금
- **quarry** 채석장
- **sunrise** 일출
- **sundown** 일몰
- **humiliate** 굴욕감을 주다, 창피를 주다
- **follower** 추종자, 신봉자
- **scatter** 흩어지게 하다, 흩뿌리다
- **international community** 국제사회
- **economic sanction** 경제적 제재
- **uphold** 유지하다, 지탱하다 (uphold-upheld-upheld)
- **smuggle** 몰래 내가다[들여오다]
- **autobiography** 자서전
- **be published** 출간되다
- **prisoner** 죄수, 재소자
- **racist** 인종 차별의, 민족주의의; 인종 차별주의자
- **regime** 정권, 체제
- **repeal** (법률을) 폐지하다

In 1980, the *Free Nelson Mandela* campaign began to bring pressure to release South Africa's most famous political prisoner. There were big events, like the music concert for his 70th birthday, when internationally known musicians gathered in support of Mandela. And inside the country there was growing violence against the racist regime. Still, another ten years passed. But on February 11th, in 1990, Nelson Mandela was finally released from prison. The apartheid laws were repealed by then President FW de Klerk.

Aha! English

But on February 11th, in 1990, Nelson Mandela was finally released from prison.
하지만 1990년 2월 11일에 넬슨 만델라는 마침내 감옥에서 풀려났다.

영어에서 연도나 달을 쓸 때 보통 앞에는 전치사 in을 써요. 하지만 on February 11th(2월 11일)처럼 특정한 날을 정해서 표현할 때는 on을 쓰죠.

ex. We celebrate the day on May 5 every year. 우리는 매년 5월 5일에 그날을 기념합니다.

Not surprisingly, the end to apartheid was not easy. Conflict and tension ruled the day, but Mandela, with calm resolve, worked tirelessly for reconciliation in South Africa. In 1993, Nelson Mandela and FW de Klerk were awarded the Nobel Peace Prize for their efforts in healing the country. And in 1994, when South Africa held its first multi-racial parliamentary elections, Nelson Mandela became the first black President.

▲ 1994년 선거때 투표하는 만델라
(By Paul Weinberg [CC BY-SA 3.0
(http://creativecommons.org/licenses/by-sa/3.0) or
GFDL (http://www.gnu.org/copyleft/fdl.html)],
via Wikimedia Commons)

Nelson Mandela achieved much as president. He introduced social and economic programs that would improve the lives of black South Africans. A new constitution was enacted that prohibited discrimination against minorities, including white people. He worked towards a goal of a united South Africa. He discouraged blacks from retaliating against old wrongs, and instead, encouraged peaceful unity among all.

- **conflict** 갈등, 물리적 충돌
- **tension** 긴장, 불안
- **resolve** 결심, 의지
- **reconciliation** 화해, 조화
- **multi-racial** 다인종의

- **parliamentary election** 총선거, 의원선거
- **enact** (법을) 제정하다, (연극 등을) 상연하다
- **minority** 소수 집단
- **discourage** 막다, 말리다
- **retaliate** 보복하다, 앙갚음하다

Even after Nelson Mandela's presidency ended in 1999, and he retired from politics in 2004, he continued to lead his people. Mandela worked for social justice and peace. He established the Nelson Mandela Foundation and The Elders, organizations devoted to ending human suffering not just in South Africa but around the world.

▲ (By Governor-General of Australia [CC BY 3.0 (http://creativecommons.org/licenses/by/3.0)], via Wikimedia Commons)

Nelson Mandela died in 2013 at the age of 95, a man who refused to let a jail cell imprison his dreams of freedom for a nation!

- **presidency** 대통령 임기
- **retire** 퇴직하다, 은퇴하다
- **foundation** 재단, 기초
- **elders** 원로들, 어른들

Comprehension Quiz

A 다음 내용이 옳으면 T, 틀리면 F에 표시하세요.

❶ Mandela studied law through an online university.   T F

❷ Mandela managed the newly formed Youth League.   T F

❸ Mandela spent 27 years imprisoned at Robben Island.   T F

❹ The government wanted to humiliate Mandela.   T F

❺ Mandela gave up protesting while he was imprisoned.   T F

B 다음 밑줄 친 부분에 들어갈 알맞은 말에 동그라미 하세요.

❶ When Mandela went underground, he went into (hiding / tunnels).

❷ Spear of the Nation blew up (prisons / railroad lines).

❸ Mandela wanted to bring the government to its (knees / senses).

❹ In 1962, Mandela was (arrested / elected) for a second time.

❺ After apartheid was abolished, Mandela did not want blacks to (retaliate / argue), or fight back against old wrongs.

Answers

A ❶ F ❷ T ❸ T ❹ T ❺ F

B ❶ hiding ❷ railroad lines ❸ senses ❹ arrested ❺ retaliate

C 다음 질문에 알맞은 답을 고르세요.

❶ What organization introduced apartheid into South Africa?

   a) the National Party

   b) the Democratic Party

   c) the African National Congress

   d) the Apartheid Agency

❷ What happened when the African National Congress was banned?

   a) Mandela and his friends decided to leave South Africa.

   b) Mandela and his friends thought the time for peaceful protest was over.

   c) Spear of the Nation captured the President of South Africa.

   d) Thankfully, apartheid ended and South Africa was at peace.

❸ What was the campaign called that brought pressure to release Mandela?

   a) *Music for Mandela*

   b) *Free Nelson Mandela*

   c) *Let Mandela Go*

   d) *Say No to Apartheid and Yes to Mandela*

Answers

C   ❶ a   ❷ b   ❸ b

Chapter Five

Mother Teresa, Saint of Calcutta

캘커타의 성인, 마더 테레사

Mother Teresa may have been small, but that never kept her from doing big things. Perhaps one of her most famous quotes was even inspired by her short stature. "Not all of us can do great things," she often said. "But we can do small things with great love."

Mother Teresa is often pictured in her blue and white sari, the simple dress-like uniform of the Missionaries of Charity. But she had been a nun long before she organized that famous convent. Her road from the schoolgirl named Anjezë Gonxhe Bojaxhiu to Saint Teresa of Calcutta was long and full of twists and turns that would take her all over the world!

▲ (By Manfredo Ferrari (Own work) [CC BY-SA 4.0 (http://creativecommons.org/licenses/by-sa/4.0)], via Wikimedia Commons)

- **Mother** 여자 수도원장, 수녀원장, 마더
- **saint** 성인, 성자
- **stature** (사람의) 키, 위상
- **sari** (인도 여성들이 입는 민속 의상) 사리
- **simple** 소박한, 평범한, 간단한
- **Missionaries of Charity** 사랑의 선교수녀회
- **convent** 수녀회, 수녀원
- **twists and turns** 우여곡절(*cf.* twist (예상 밖의) 전개)

Her journey began when she left her home in Skopje, in the
Republic of Macedonia, to join the Sisters of Loreto in Ireland to
become a missionary. But first, she had to learn English so that
she could teach in India. She studied hard and when she was
just nineteen, she traveled to Darjeeling, near the Himalayan
Mountains, and began to teach at St. Teresa's school. It was
here that she would choose the name that today has such
worldwide recognition.

Young women studying in a convent take a series of vows
before they become nuns. When young Anjezë made her first
religious promise, she wanted the name of Saint Therese of
Lisieux, also known as the Little Flower of Jesus. But she could
not take the name Therese since another nun already had that
name. So she chose the Spanish spelling, Teresa, instead.
When she took her final vows in 1937, as was the tradition,
she took the title "Mother" and became known from then on as
Mother Teresa.

- **journey** 여정, 여행
- **Republic of Macedonia** 마케도니아공화국
- **Sisters of Loreto** 로레토 수녀회(*cf.* sister 수녀, 자매)
- **missionary** 선교사
- **recognition** 인식, 인정
- **take a vow** 맹세하다, 서원하다
- **a series of** 일련의
- **Lisieux** 리지외(테레사 성녀가 살았던 프랑스 북서부의 도시)
- **minister to** ~을 보살피다, ~에 도움이 되다
- **Bengali** 벵골인, 벵골어; 벵골(사람, 말)의
- **Hindi** 힌디어(인도 북부에서 사용되는 인도 공용어의 하나)
- **famine** 기근, 굶주림
- **despair** 절망, 실망
- **calling** 하느님의 부르심, 소명 (의식)

Mother Teresa next taught at St. Mary's High School for Girls, a school that ministered to some of the poorest in Calcutta. Through education, she hoped to ease the suffering of these Bengali girls. Mother Teresa even learned to speak Bengali and Hindi to better communicate with her young charges. In 1944, she became the principal of the school, and though she was distressed at the poverty, famine, violence and despair she witnessed in the city, it seemed as if Mother Teresa's life of service was complete. But then she experienced what she described as "a calling within a calling."

It was 1946, and Mother Teresa was on a train, on her way to a retreat, when she heard Christ speak to her. He told her that she should leave the school and go to work among some of the city's poorest people, in the slums of Calcutta. She was nearly forty years old, but she did not question her calling, even though it took nearly two years for her to convince the convent to let her go. And even when she was allowed to leave, Mother Teresa did not have a clear idea of what she needed to do.

She traded in her habit for a white and blue sari and decided that for the next six months, she would study basic medical training. Then she entered the slums, her only desire was to ease the suffering of the "poorest of the poor" in Calcutta.

It was not an easy task, and many times, Mother Teresa longed to return to the comfort of the old convent. But she refused to give up, even when she was forced to beg for food and supplies herself. She opened a school in the slums and established a home for the dying and poor. Finally, in 1950, she received permission from the Vatican for an order that she called the Missionaries of Charity. It was just a small group, made up of just a few women, mostly former students and teachers from St. Mary's, her former high school. But from this small beginning grew something bigger than Mother Teresa could have ever imagined!

▲ (By flowcomm (Flickr: Missionaries of Charity Mother House) [CC BY 2.0 (http://creativecommons.org/licenses/by/2.0)], via Wikimedia Commons)

- **retreat** 피정(일상생활에서 벗어나 수도원 같은 곳에서 묵상이나 기도를 하는 일)
- **Christ** 예수 그리스도
- **slum** (도시) 빈민가
- **convince** 설득하다, 납득시키다
- **trade in A for B** A를 (웃돈을 얹어 주고) B로 바꾸다
- **basic medical training** 기초 의료 훈련
- **desire** 욕구, 갈망

- **many times** 여러 번
- **long** 간절히 바라다
- **comfort** 안락, 편안
- **beg for** ~을 간청하다[구하다]
- **supplies** 물자, 보급품
- **permission** 허가, 허락
- **make up for** ~로 구성하다

She and her sisters would minister to thousands upon thousands of people all over the world. In her own words, they cared for "the hungry, the naked, the homeless, the crippled, the blind, the lepers, all those people who feel unwanted, unloved, uncared for throughout society, people that have become a burden to the society and are shunned by everyone." This mission became orphanages, hospices for those with AIDS, help for refugees, a colony for lepers, and mobile clinics, too. Her charitable work gained attention, and soon, donations poured in so that Mother Teresa could provide homes and help far beyond Calcutta.

As her mission grew, more and more women joined her. Her sisters traveled to Asia, the Americas, Europe, and Africa to help the poor. And wherever they went, they ministered in the faith of those they served. Whether Hindu or Muslim, atheist or Catholic, it made no difference to the Missionaries of Charity. Soon, the sisters were joined by the Missionaries of Charity Brothers and scores of lay volunteers. She was awarded the Jewel of India, the highest honor an Indian civilian can receive. In 1979, Mother Teresa was awarded the Nobel Peace Prize for her work "in bringing help to suffering humanity."

- **thousands upon thousands** 수천 수만
- **care for** ~을 보살피다
- **naked** 벌거벗은, 옷을 입지 않은
- **crippled** 불구의, 무능력한
- **leper** 나환자, 한센병 환자
- **unwanted** 원치 않는, 환영받지 못하는
- **uncared for** 보살핌을 못 받는
- **burden** 짐, 부담
- **shun** 피하다, 멀리하다
- **orphanage** 고아원
- **hospice** 호스피스(말기 환자들을 위한 병원)

- **AIDS** 에이즈, 후천성 면역 결핍증
- **refugee** 난민, 망명자
- **colony** 격리 시설, 집단 거주지
- **mobile clinic** 이동 진료소
- **charitable** 자비로운, 자선의
- **gain attention** 주의를 끌다
- **donation** 기부, 기증
- **atheist** 무신론자
- **make no difference** 차이가 없다
- **scores of** 많은
- **lay** 평신도의, 일반의

Aha! English

In her own words, they cared for "the hungry, the naked, the homeless, the crippled, the blind, the lepers, ~." 그녀의 말로는 그들은 '굶주린 사람들, 헐벗은 사람들, 집이 없는 사람들, 장애가 있는 사람들, 앞을 못 보는 사람들, 나환자들, ~'을 보살폈다.

'the + 형용사'는 '~한 사람들'이라는 뜻이에요. 따라서 이것은 '형용사 + people'로 바꿔 쓸 수 있어요.

ex. The rich(= Rich people) are not always happier than the poor(= poor people). 부자들이 가난한 사람들보다 항상 더 행복한 것은 아니다.

Despite years of poor health, Mother Teresa continued to lead her sisters and travel globally to serve the poor and dying. But on September 5, 1997, the tiny nun's big heart finally gave out. And yet, that was not the end of Mother Teresa's story. There would be another twist or two in her long journey.

▲ 스코페에 있는 마더 테레사 기념관

After her death, Mother Teresa's journal writings became public, and in her writings, she often expressed her doubts about her faith. But instead of people losing faith, they were inspired! Mother Teresa's doubts only demonstrated her strong bond with the simple people she came to serve, a bond that would eventually lead to her sainthood!

POP QUIZ

How did Mother Teresa's journal writings affect the world?

ⓐ Her doubts inspired all those who had doubts as well.
ⓑ Her doubts caused many people to stop supporting her.

ⓐ 답정

* **give out** 정지하다, 멈추다, 힘이 빠지다　　* **become public** 세상에 알려지다　　* **sainthood** 성인의 신분

In death, as in her life, Mother Teresa administered aid to the sick and suffering. In 2002, the Vatican, the governing head of the Roman Catholic Church, recognized the first miracle attributed to Mother Teresa in 1998. A woman in India had been cured of a tumor after praying for Mother Teresa's help. Thirteen years later, Pope Francis recognized the second Mother Teresa miracle when a Brazilian man with a viral brain infection was cured in 2008 after his family prayed to her.

On September 4, 2016, tens of thousands of people gathered in Rome to attend the canonization of the woman often called "the saint of the gutters" because of her work with the poor. Today, she is known as Saint Teresa of Calcutta, a saint who did great things with great love!

- **as in** ~의 경우(에서)와 같이
  (*cf.* in death as in life 살아 있을 때와 같이 사후에도)
- **administer** 주다, 관리하다, 실행하다
- **governing** 관리하는
- **attribute to** ~의 덕분으로 돌리다
- **tumor** 종양
- **pope** 교황

- **Brazilian** 브라질의
- **viral** 바이러스에 의한
- **infection** 감염
- **tens of thousands** 수천 수만(개)의, 수많은
- **canonization** 시성(식), 성전 승인
- **gutter** 빈민굴, 도랑

Aha! Culture

canonization 시성식

가톨릭에서는 순교했거나 생전에 특별히 훌륭한 선교활동 등을 해서 덕이 높은 사람들을 성인으로 추대하는데, 이렇게 추대된 인물을 성인으로 선언하는 의식을 '시성식'이라고 해요. 교황청에서 시성 요청이 올라온 인물을 자세히 조사한 후에 교황에게 보고하면, 교황이 그를 인정하는 발표를 하죠.

Have you found all the qualities of a great leader among these pages? Compassion, courage, ingenuity, and persistence are a few of them, aren't they? Perhaps you could name even more traits in Queen Victoria and Napoleon, Gandhi and Nelson Mandela, and even Mother Teresa. But one thing is certain. These men and women did not start out to change the world. They saw a great need and acted, not understanding what a difference they would make. You, too, can develop the characteristics of great leadership, and who can know what a difference *you* might make in the world!

▪ compassion 연민, 동정심

▪ ingenuity 독창성, 기발한 재주

Comprehension Quiz

A 다음 내용이 옳으면 T, 틀리면 F에 표시하세요.

❶ Mother Teresa was known to be a tall woman. `T` `F`

❷ Mother Teresa believed everyone could do small things with great love. `T` `F`

❸ As a schoolgirl, Mother Teresa wore a blue and white uniform. `T` `F`

❹ Mother Teresa spent her whole life in her hometown. `T` `F`

❺ Mother Teresa's mission became orphanages and mobile clinics. `T` `F`

B 다음 밑줄 친 부분에 들어갈 알맞은 말에 동그라미 하세요.

❶ It was very (easy / difficult) for Mother Teresa to help the poor.

❷ Mother Teresa herself had to (beg / steal) in order to survive.

❸ Mother Teresa finally opened a school in the (slums / city).

❹ Mother Teresa received permission from the (Vatican / government) for an order.

Answers

A ❶ F ❷ T ❸ F ❹ F ❺ T

B ❶ difficult ❷ beg ❸ slums ❹ Vatican

C 다음 질문에 알맞은 답을 고르세요.

❶ Why is Mother Teresa given the title "Mother"?

   a) It's traditional for nuns to take the title after their final vows.

   b) All nuns who are teachers are called "Mother."

   c) She was the oldest nun and other girls looked up to her.

   d) She'd had a child before she entered the convent.

❷ What did Mother Teresa do before entering the slums of Calcutta?

   a) She gave away all her books and teaching materials.

   b) She traded in her habit for a red and white sari.

   c) She begged for money and food for the poor.

   d) She studied basic medical training.

❸ What awards were given to Mother Teresa?

   a) the Jewel of Macedonia and the Nobel Peace Prize

   b) the Prize for Peace and the Gem of India

   c) the Jewel of India and the Nobel Peace Prize

   d) the Nobel Peace Prize and the International Prize for Humanity

Let's Review the Story

빈칸을 채우며 이야기를 다시 정리해 보세요.

Title: Great ___________ of the World

Queen Victoria: She holds the record for being the second longest reigning m________ in Britain. She and her husband brought many reforms to the people, but after Prince A________ death, Victoria went into m________ for 25 years. Still, she served her country well and her reign became known as the G________ Age of Empire, bringing the country peace and prosperity.

Napoleon Bonaparte: He was both a m________ and political leader who changed not only F________ but also the world. He conquered many countries and built an empire before his final defeat at the Battle of W________. Napoleon died in exile, but the democratic ideals of his ________ Code live on today.

Mahatma Gandhi: When he was forced to leave a train in S________ A________, he set out to change the system. He called for protest s________ and encouraged the practice of p________ r________. When he returned home, he worked for Indian i________, and though jailed and eventually assassinated, Gandhi succeeded in bringing much needed changes to I________.

Nelson Mandela: He had a spirit for f________! When the policy of a________ became law in his country, he protested so much that he was imprisoned for 27 years on ________ Island. At last released, he became the first ________ President of South Africa, bringing peace, equality, and freedom for all the people.

Mother Teresa: The tiny nun believed that everyone could do "________ things with great ________." She left home to become a m________, but Christ called her to live in the s________, helping the poor. She started a new order, the M________ of Charity, and today, the work of Saint Teresa of Calcutta continues all over the world.

Let's Think & Talk

아래의 물음에 대해 생각해 보고 자유롭게 답하세요.

❶ 이 책에 나온 지도자들의 업적에는 어떤 것들이 있는지 각각 정리해서 이야기해 보세요.

❷ 이 책에 나온 지도자들의 공통점과 차이점이 무엇인지 살펴보세요. 공통적인 특징을 가진 지도자들은 누구이고, 어떤 점이 비슷한지 이야기해 보세요.

❸ 이 책에 나온 지도자 중에서 여러분이 가장 존경하는 사람은 누구인가요? 그 사람을 선택한 이유를 이야기해 보세요.

❹ 여러분이 알고 있는 또 다른 위대한 지도자가 있나요? 그의 삶과 업적에 대해 조사하고, 정리해서 이야기해 보세요.

Let's Review the Story

Title: Great **Leaders** of the World

Queen Victoria: She holds the record for being the second longest reigning **monarch** in Britain. She and her husband brought many reforms to the people, but after Prince **Albert's** death, Victoria went into **mourning** for 25 years. Still, she served her country well and her reign became known as the **Golden** Age of Empire, bringing the country peace and prosperity.

Napoleon Bonaparte: He was both a **military** and political leader who changed not only **France** but also the world. He conquered many countries and built an empire before his final defeat at the Battle of **Waterloo**. Napoleon died in exile, but the democratic ideals of his **Napoleonic** Code live on today.

Mahatma Gandhi: When he was forced to leave a train in **South Africa**, he set out to change the system. He called for protest **strikes** and encouraged the practice of **passive resistance**. When he returned home, he worked for Indian **independence**, and though jailed and eventually assassinated, Gandhi succeeded in bringing much needed changes to **India**.

Nelson Mandela: He had a spirit for **freedom**! When the policy of **apartheid** became law in his country, he protested so much that he was imprisoned for 27 years on **Robben** Island. At last released, he became the first **black** President of South Africa, bringing peace, equality, and freedom for all the people.

Mother Teresa: The tiny nun believed that everyone could do " **small** things with great **love**." She left home to become a **missionary**, but Christ called her to live in the **slums**, helping the poor. She started a new order, the **Missionaries** of Charity, and today, the work of Saint Teresa of Calcutta continues all over the world.

Great Leaders of the World

전문 번역

세계의 위대한 지도자들

Great Leaders of the World

p.10~11

만일 18세기, 19세기, 또는 20세기의 세계에서 가장 위대한 지도자의 이름을 대라고 한다면, 여러분은 누구를 말하겠는가? 여러분은 정치적 통치자, 왕, 여왕, 또는 황제를 선택하겠는가? 아니 어쩌면 여러분은 인도주의자나 산업의 선구자, 세계적인 발명가, 또는 심지어 정신적인 지도자를 고를지도 모르겠다. 하지만 여러분이 누구를 뽑든지, 여러분은 아마도 여러분이 선택한 위대한 지도자가 다른 사람들이 고른 이들과 많은 공통적인 특성을 지니고 있었다는 사실을 알게 될 것이다.

위대한 지도자들은 비슷한 특징들을 가지고 있는 경향이 있다. 그들은 보통 야심 차고 자신감이 있지만, 그래도 여전히 겸손하고 동정심이 있는 본성을 가지고 있다. 그들은 예지자들이다. 즉, 그들은 미래를 창조적으로 본다. 위대한 지도자에게서는 또 비록 항상 그것이 군대를 전투로 이끄는 그러한 종류의 용기는 아니지만 용기를 발견할 거라고 기대하라. 그리고 불굴의 의지를 잊지 마라. 이들은 그들에게 불리하게 조작된 역경에도 불구하고 멈추기를 거부하는 남녀들이다!

p.12~13

위대한 지도자들은 선구자이자 스승이고, 사상가들이며, 비록 그들에게 결점들이 있을지 모르지만 그들은 항상 미래 세대들을 위해서 세상을 보다 나은 쪽으로 남겨 둘 것이다. 감사하게도, 세계를 보다 나

은 쪽으로 바꿔왔던 많은 위대한 근대의 지도자들이 있어서 딱 한 사람의 이름만 대는 것은 정말로 어려울 것이다. 대신에 지난 몇 세기 동안의 다섯 명의 지도자들을 더 자세히 살펴보자. 오랜 삶을 살았던 여왕, 결연했던 황제, 놀라운 저항가, 열정적인 대통령, 그리고 한 명의 아주 왜소했던 수녀에 대해 알아본 다음에, 여러분이 그들 모두가 공유하고 있는 특징들을 말할 수 있는지 보자!

p.14~15

살아있는 동안에 빅토리아 여왕은 영국 역사에서 어떤 군주보다 가장 긴 통치 기간을 가졌었다. 심지어 오늘날에도 그녀는 영국의 왕과 여왕들을 통틀어 두 번째로 오랫동안 통치한 군주라는 기록을 보유하고 있다. 비록 그것이 주목할 만한 것이긴 하지만 그녀의 오랜 통치 기간이 빅토리아를 위대한 지도자로 만들어준 것은 아니다. 여왕인 이 할머니에게는 단순히 그녀가 왕위에 있었던 여러 해보다 훨씬 더 많은 게 있었다! 거의 유아기 때부터 빅토리아는 여왕이 될 운명이었다. 그러다 보니 그녀의 어머니와 어머니의

친한 친구인 존 콘로이는 그녀를 엄격한 규칙 아래에서 키웠다. 숨이 막혀서 그녀는 막 13세가 되었을 때 일기를 쓰기 시작했다. 일기에다 빅토리아는 그녀가 좋아한 것을 무엇이든 쓰고 말할 수 있었는데, 이런 일상적인 습관은 그녀가 죽기 열흘 전까지 계속되었다!

p.16~17

18세의 어린 나이에 왕위에 올랐을 때, 빅토리아는 즉각 그녀 자신의 의견을 주장했다. 그녀는 자신의 어머니를 궁전 건너편에 있는 방에서 살도록 보냈다. 그리고 어머니의 친구인 존 콘로이에 관해서는, 그가 빅토리아의 인생에 끼어드는 것을 금지했고, 그를 절대 다시는 보지 않았다. 대신에 그녀는 수상인 멜버른 경에게 의지하여, 그가 그녀에게 조언하고 가르치도록 했다. 빅토리아의 대관식 시기에는 왕위에 대한 영국 사람들의 지지가 최저치였고, 그래서 새 여왕은 아주 힘들었다. 비록 초창기에는 실수를 했지만, 멜버른 경의 꾸준한 도움으로 어린 빅토리아는 군주가 되는 것이 무엇인지 점점 배워나갔다. 그리고 그렇게 함으로써 그녀는 국민들의 신뢰를 얻었다.

p.18~19

하지만 1840년에 빅토리아는 독일 왕자인 앨버트와 결혼했다. 수상은 앨버트의 영향력이 높아지고 있는 한편 자신의 영향력은 끝나가고 있다는 사실을 알았다. 비록 빅토리아가 스스로 의지가 강한 것은 분명했

음에도 불구하고, 그녀는 앨버트에게 크게 의존했다. 이러한 의존과 충성의 패턴은 빅토리아가 그녀에게 매우 유용한 도움을 제공하는 사람들과 깊고 신뢰할 만한 관계를 발전시키면서 그녀의 통치 기간 내내 계속되었다. 하지만 영국 사람들이 앨버트 공을 시작으로, 신뢰받았던 이 조력자들을 늘 좋아했던 것은 아니었다. 이것이 그에 대한 여왕의 마음을 변화시키지는 않았다. 그

녀는 완전히 그에게 헌신했고, 진심으로 그의 관심사들을 지지했는데, 이것들은 궁극적으로는 영국에는 아주 좋은 결과로 나타났다. 1851년에 예술과 과학, 그리고 산업에 대한 앨버트의 관심은 그가 대영 박람회를 조직하도록 만들었는데, 이것은 그 행사가 임시로 열렸던 주요 건물 때문에 수정궁 박람회라고도 불렸다. 국제 행상들은 그들의 상품을 가져와 이 세계 박람회에 전시했고, 그것은 꽤 인상적인 성공을 거뒀다. 6개월 동안 6백만 명 이상의 사람들이 런던에 있던 그 장소를 방문했다! 수익금은 나중에 산업과 문화 박물관들을 위한 땅을 사는 데 사용되었는데, 그 건물들에는 오늘날 세계에서 가장 유명한 박물관들도 몇 곳 포함되어 있다.

p.20~21

세계에서 가장 큰 장식 미술 박물관인 빅토리아 & 앨버트 박물관은 12.5 에이커에 이른다. 그리고 영국의 주요 관광지 중 하나인 과학 박물관에는 매년 수천 명의 영국 학생들이 방문한다. 그리고 이들 박물관과 다른 박물관들의 본거지인, 켄싱턴의 엑셔비션 로드에 오는 어떤 방문객이든 우뚝 솟아 있는 공룡의 해골들을 보기 위해 국립 역사 박물관 안을 둘러보게 될 게 틀림없다!

그러나 빅토리아의 지원은 박물관들의 건물을 훨씬 넘어섰다. 그녀는 발명가, 건축가, 그리고 과학자들을 격려했다. 그녀는 또한 영향력뿐만 아니라 지금도 제공하는 훌륭한 후원자였다. 위대한 동식물 연구가인 찰스 다윈을 포함하여 여왕이 살던 시대의 많은 주목할 만한 인물들이 빅토리아의 지원으로 혜택을 받았다.

p.22~23

슬프게도, 빅토리아의 인생은 이 시기 즈음 급격하게 변했다. 그녀의 사랑하는 남편 앨버트가 1861년 12월에 장티푸스로 죽었다. 앨버트는 군주로서의 그녀의 인생에 강력한 영향력을 가지고 있었고, 빅토

리아는 엄청난 충격을 받았다. 그녀의 슬픔은 너무 깊어서 빅토리아는 그다음 25년 동안 검은색 옷을 입었다! 하지만 사람들이 생각했듯이 그녀가 남편의 죽음을 따라 궁정의 생활에서 사라져버린 것은 아니었다. 빅토리아는 애도 중임에도 불구하고 그녀의 왕족으로서의 임무를 계속해 나갔다. 그녀는 계속해서 서신을 왕래했고, 장관이나 다른 공무원들에게 알현을 허가했다. 그렇기는 하지만 사람들은 그녀가 일상적으로 보이지 않아 괴로워했고, 그녀가 돈을 벌지 않고 있다(일을 하지 않고 있다)는 불평들이 있었다.

p.24~25

그녀는 매우 공개적인 등장을 위해 남편의 사망 10주기를 선택했다. 그녀의 아들인 웨일스 왕자는 그의 아버지를 죽음으로 몰고 갔던 것과 같은 병인 장티푸스에서 기적적으로 회복했다. 빅토리아는 1871년에 세인트 폴 대성당에서 열린 그를 위한 추수감사절 미사에 참석했다. 그 등

장으로 그녀는 국민들 마음속으로 다시 다가가기 위해 노력하기 시작했다. 하지만 그녀의 가족은 여왕과 그렇게 행복하지는 않았다. 그들은 빅토리아와 존 브라운이라는 스코틀랜드 사람이자 하인 사이의 우정에 대해 점점 걱정하게 되었다. 그들은 브라운의 영향력과 그에 대한 빅토리아의 강한 충심에 대해 걱정했다. 이 일은 다시 한번 군주제에 강하게 반대하는 유럽에서의 정서에 도움이 되지 않았다.

빅토리아의 수상인 벤저민 디즈레일리는 여왕을 위

한 새로운 계획으로 가지고 돕고 나섰다. 1877년, 그는 그녀가 인도의 여제로 명명되어야 한다고 결정했다. 비록 인도가 1858년 이후부터 왕국의 한 부분이긴 했지만, 빅토리아의 새 지위는 그 연대를 강화했고 그녀의 인기는 폭발했다! 존 브라운은 몇 년 후에 죽었고, 빅토리아는 영국이 세계에서 가장 강력한 국가가 되어 가는 것을 지켜보았다.

p.26~27

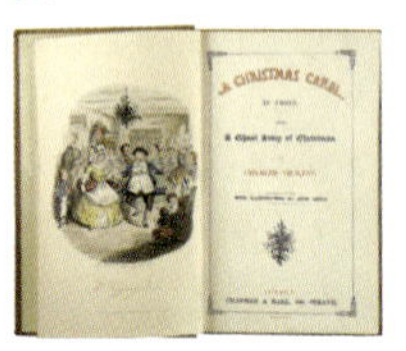

그럼에도 불구하고 빅토리아의 국가에는 또 다른 측면이 있었는데, 이것은 당시의 인기 작가인 찰스 디킨스가 그의 많은 소설에 썼던 삶의 모습이었다. 빈곤은 1800년대 내내 문제였는데, 특히 영국이 농촌 경제에서 산업 혁명으로 넘어가면서 그러했다. 결국에 빅토리아의 통치 기간에 인구가 두 배 이상 늘었다. 어른들뿐만 아니라 많은 어린이가 일했다. 하지만 디킨스의 〈크리스마스 캐럴〉과 같은 작품들에 그려져 있던 모습에도 불구하고, 빅토리아는 가난한 사람들의 고통을 덜어 주는 여러 개혁들을 책임지고 있었다.

예를 들어, *예방 접종법*에 대해 생각해 보면, 그것은 무료 예방 접종을 이용할 수 있게 했다. 혹은 *철도 규제법*에는 가난한 사람들이 더 적당한 가격으로 여행하도록 하는 조항이 들어

있었다. 사실, 그녀의 지원 덕택에 1863년에 철도와 런던 지하철이 세워졌다. 그리고 여왕이 여덟 번째 아이를 낳을 동안 클로로폼을 사용했을 때, 이 강력

한 마취제의 사용은 널리 퍼지게 되었다. 더는 여자들이 고통스러운 자연 분만으로 고생하지 않아도 되었는데, 왜냐하면 어쨌든 빅토리아 여왕 자신이 그 약을 사용했기 때문이었다!

p.28~29

다른 변화들도 있었다. 그녀의 재임 동안의 정부 개혁들 때문에 영국은 유럽이 겪고 있던 정치적인 대변동을 많이 피했다. 왕국은 캐나다, 호주, 그리고 아프리카 일부와 인도뿐만 아니라 남태평양을 포함하면서 크기가 두 배로 늘었다. 영국 제국에서는 태양이 절대 지지 않는다는 말이 들렸고, 빅토리아는 확실히 아주 오랫동안 그 말이 진실로 남아있게 하였다.

1901년 1월에 여왕이 죽었을 때, 그녀는 63년 동안 통치를 했었다! 그녀의 장례식 요구사항들은 흥미로우면서도 자세했다. 그녀는 그녀가 사랑한 앨버트 공이 손에 했던 깁스뿐만 아니라 그의 가운도 그녀와 함께 묻어달라고 요청했다. 그녀는 또한 그녀의 충직한 하인이었던 존 브라운을 기억했다. 그의 한 타래의 머리카락도 그녀와 함께 묻혔다. 122권이나 되는 그녀의 일기에 대해서는 그녀의 딸인 베아트리체가 유저 관리자로 명명되었는데, 그녀는 어머니의 바람들을 수행하는 책임을 지게 되었다. 그녀는 여왕의 많은 글들을 조사했고, 비록 그녀가 여왕의 말들을 편집했고, 많은 페이지가 심지어 불타기도 했지만, 빅토리아 여왕이 썼던 많은 것들은 오늘날에도 남아있다. 그녀의 글들은 세계가 1800년대 대부분 동안에 군주가 된다는 것이 어떤 의미였는지를 들여다보게 한다.

p.30~31

놀랍게도 빅토리아의 영향력은 그녀의 죽음과 함께 끝나지 않았다. 그녀의 아홉 명 자녀들의 결혼은 유럽 전역에서 중요한 유대 관계를 형성했다. 그녀의 42명에 이르는 손주들은 그 후로도 오랫동안 왕조

를 보장했다. 그래서 빅토리아는 '유럽의 할머니'라는 칭호를 얻었다.

역사의 어떤 한 기간 전체가 누군가의 이름으로 불리는 것이 일상적인 일은 아니다. 하지만 빅토리아는 키가 단지 5피트에 불과했지만, 군주 중에서도 우뚝 솟은 존재였다. 그리고 인구 팽창과 경제적인 어려움에도 불구하고, 빅토리아 시대는 평화와 번영으로 잘 알려져 왔다. 이 여왕의 매우 길었던 통치 기간은 비록 처음에는 흔들렸지만, 그 군주와 함께 군주제가 번영하고 국민들도 번영하면서 제국의 전성기로 기억된다!

2장. 단호한 군사 천재, 나폴레옹 보나파르트

p.34~35

나폴레옹 보나파르트는 포기를 모르는 남자였다. 그는 "내 사전에 불가능이라는 말은 없다"는 유명한 말을 했다. 몇 번이고 계속해서, 이 프랑스 장군이자 정치 지도자는 패할 것이 분명해 보였지만, 결국 훌륭히 다시 일어났다! 나폴레옹은 1769년에 코르시카 섬에서 태어났는데, 이탈리아 땅에 속한 이 작은 부분이 프랑스 통치하에 들어간 지 겨우 일 년 후였다. 별로 놀라운 일도 아니지만, 그가 프랑스 본토에 있는 사관 학교에 다녔을 때, 그는 새 나라의 관습에 대해 아는 게 거의 없는 아웃사이더였다. 58명 중 47등이었던 졸업반에서의 그의 등수를 보면, 그 누구도 이 학생이 세계에서 가장 위대한 군 지도자 중 한 명이 될 것이라고 예상하지

못했을 것이다!

p.36~37
하지만 그의 경력이 시작될 때, 나폴레옹의 마음은 고향과 함께 있었다. 그는 프랑스 지배에서 자유로운, 독립된 코르시카를 열망했다. 그래서 그는 섬으로 돌아와 전략을 공부하면서 시간을 보내며 행동할 때를 기다렸다. 1789년 그해에 프랑스 혁명은 이미 격렬한 변화를 프랑스 본토 정부에 가져왔다. 하지만 코르시카에서의 나폴레옹의 노력은 결코 순조롭게 출발하지 못했다. 그래서 군인으로서 성공하기로 결심한 이 젊은 군인은 그의 섬을 떠나 프랑스에 있는 새 정부에 협력했다. 그리고 나폴레옹은 절대 뒤를 돌아보지 않았다.

그는 군대에서 빠르게 진급했다. 24세의 나이로 그는 준장으로 진급했고, 이탈리아의 프랑스 군대를 책임지게 되었다. 나폴레옹은 새 정부의 성쇠 동안 계속해서 성장했다. 지금은 집정부로 알려진 그 공화국은 1795년에 왕정주의자의 반란에 직면했다. 수적으로 극히 열세였음에도 불구하고, 나폴레옹

과 그의 군대는 반란을 물리쳤다. 그는 겨우 26세였고, 즉시 소장으로 진급했다!

p.38~39
나폴레옹의 아주 높은 야망들은 그의 계급과 맞아 떨어져 갔다. 그는 다음에 영국 침략이라는 임무를 맡았다. 그의 해군이 영국 해군을 물리칠 수 없다는 것은 알고 있었기 때문에, 나폴레옹은 대신 인도로

이어지는 영국 무역로를 끊을 수 있도록 이집트를 침략할 것을 제안했다. 그는 1798년 피라미드 전투에서의 결정적 승리를 만끽했다. 그리고 나서 1799년, 프랑스로 돌아갈 기회를 엿보면서 나폴레옹은 이집트를 떠나 집정부

에 맞서 싸울 준비를 했다!

나폴레옹은 새 집정관 중 한 명인 에마뉘엘 시에예스와 권력 탈취를 위해 힘을 합쳤고, 쿠데타는 성공했다. 집정부는 3명의 통령으로 교체됐고, 나폴레옹이 제1통령이 되었다. 그가 군사 전략가 이상으로 이름을 떨쳤던 것은 이 시기 동안이었다. 나폴레옹은 강력한 정치 지도자로서도 역시 뛰어났다.

p.40~41
그는 사람들의 요구를 이해했다. 나폴레옹은 사람들이 나라의 내전과 혼란에 지쳐있다는 사실을 알고 있었다. 제1통령으로서, 그는 혁명 후의 프랑스에 안정을 회복시키기로 했다. 그는 또한 자유와 평등을 포함하고 있는 프랑스 혁명의 많은 이상을 받아들였다. 이러한 특성들을 마음속에 품고서 그는 새롭고 더 개선된 공화국 헌법을 제안했다. 이것은 종교의 자유와 부모의 재산과 직위를 그들의 자녀에게 물려주는 세습 특권을 끝내는 것을 규정하고 있었다. 이것은 유럽의 봉건 체제에서는 일반적인 관습이었다. 새 헌법 아래서는, *모든* 인간은 평등할 것이었다!

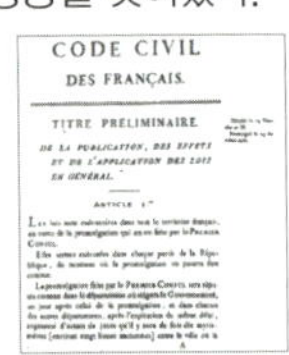

그런데 나폴레옹은 프랑스에 많은 개혁을 가져온 다른 종류의 활동을 시작했다. 파리의 끔찍하게 불결한 상태는 매력적인 공원과 가로수가 늘어진 도로들이 있는 아름다운 도시로 변화됐다. 그는 오늘날에도 여전히 사용되고 있는 더 나은 은행 체계를 설립했다. 하지만 아마도 가장 오래 지속되고 있고, 가장 인상적인 그의 유산은 나폴레옹 법전이다.

p.42~43
나폴레옹은 그의 법전에 대한 큰 뜻이 있었을까? 말하기 어려운데, 왜냐하면 그 당시에 그는 그저 난장판이었던 프랑스 법률 체계를 청소하기를 원했었기 때문이다. 프랑스에는 관습들이 있었고, 이것들은 마을마다 달랐기 때문에 정말 법률은 없었다. 특권과 특별한 혜택들은 봉건 영주들과 왕들에게 주어져 있

었다. 다른 지역들에서 이런 유형의 특권들이 없어지는 동안에도 법체계는 바뀌지 않았다. 그래서 나폴레옹과 그의 위원회는 사법체계를 단순화하기 위해 열심히 일했다. 그들은 나라 전체를 위한 일련의 법률을 제정했다. 이전 법들은 라틴어로 쓰인 로마의 법규에 기초한 것이었다. 그런데 이 법률은 프랑스어로 쓰였고, 그래서 사람들은 그 법률들을 이해할 수 있었다.

나폴레옹 법전의 핵심은 평등이었다. 더 이상 한쪽으로 치우치는 일은 없을 것이었고, 이러한 이상은 전 세계로 퍼져나갔는데, 왜냐하면 나폴레옹이 아주 많은 다른 나라를 정복했기 때문이다. 나폴레옹 법전은 그를 따라 이탈리아, 네덜란드, 그리고 벨기에, 캐나다와 사우디아라비아까지 내내 따라다녔다. 이들 나라에서 프랑스 민법의 민주적인 영향력을 발견하기는 쉽다. 나폴레옹은 평등을 본국으로 가져오려고 노력하면서, 그가 유럽 대부분을 정복했을 때 목격된 적 있는 가장 큰 군대 중 하나를 만들어냈다. 그의 노력들은 후한 보상을 받았다. 나폴레옹은 1802년에 종신통령이 되었다.

p.44~45

하지만 그의 성공은 그의 적들을 유인하는 데만 일조했다. 이 사람들은 나폴레옹의 새로운 체제에 찬성하지 않았고 그를 암살하기로 했다. 그들의 계획들은 좌절되었지만, 나폴레옹은 1804년에 자신에 대한 결정을 내렸다. 그는 스스로 황제 자리에 오르기로 했고, 그래서 유럽의 다른 적들은 세계의 지도자를 암살하는 것에 대해 다시 한번 생각해보게 됐다!

평등이라는 이상을 중요하게 여기고 프

랑스 혁명의 신념들을 껴안았던 한 남자가 황제로서 모든 사람을 지배하기로 선택해야 했던 것은 이상한 것처럼 보일 수 있다. 하지만 나폴레옹은 항상 야심으로 가득 찼던 사람이었고, 게다가 사람들은 그를 전폭적으로 지지했다. 그의 더 작은 규모의 군대가 1805년에 러시아와 오스트리아라는 세계에서 가장 강력했던 두 나라를 물리쳤을 때, 그 황제에 대한 의심은 없었을 것이다. 나폴레옹은 자신이 유럽에서 가장 유능한 군 지도자라는 것을 스스로 증명했다.

p.46~47

하지만 그의 성공에도 불구하고 나폴레옹은 여전히 성취하고 싶은 것이 많았다. 그는 쉽게 포기하지 않는 남자였다는 사실을 기억해라. 그래서 사랑하는 아내인 조제핀이 그에게 후계자를 낳아주지 못하자 그는 1810년에 그녀와 이혼했다. 그는 마리 루이즈와 결혼했고, 얼마 지나지 않아, 역시 나폴레옹이라고 불린 아들을 얻었다. 군사 전선에서 나폴레옹은 러시아를 침략하는, 불행으로 끝나게 될 결정을 해버렸다. 그는 60만 명 이상을 데리고 6월에 러시아로 갔고, 결국에 모스크바를 점령하기는 했으나 그것은 너무 긴 작전이었다. 몹시 추운 겨울이 나폴레옹 군대를 이겼다. 그가 프랑스로 돌아왔을 때, 그에게는 가까스로 3만 명이 남아 있었다. 나폴레옹의 오랜 적들인 오스트리아와 프로이센 군의 연합군들이 이 황제의 인력 손실을 이용하여 파리에 진격했다. 나폴레옹은 퇴위하고 그의 왕권을 루이 18세에게 물려줬다. 한때 천하무적이었던 이 황제는 1814년 3월에 엘바 섬으로 유배되었다. 하지만 그는 그곳에서 오래 머물지는 않았다.

나폴레옹은 엘바 섬에서 때를 기다리며 충실한 지지자들로부터 정보를 모으고 있었다. 프랑스는 불안했고, 한때 황제였던 그는 자신의 나라를 되찾을 수 있다고 믿었다. 1815년 3월, 그는 섬에서의 대담한 탈출 계획을 세웠다. 단 1년 만에 나폴레옹은 되돌아 왔다. 그는 환호를 받으며 파리로 입성했고, 왕인 루이 18세는 피신을 해야만 했다.

p.48~49

하지만 '불가능'이라는 단어를 믿지 않던 이 남자에게 그것은 짧은 성공이었다. 비록 그가 그의 편으로 인상적인 군대를 모으기는 했지만, 다른 유럽 군대들은 그에게 대항해서 결집했다. 나폴레옹은 이번에는 워털루 전투에서 다시 싸우기로 했다. 나폴레옹은 그의 오랜 적인 웰링턴과 벨기에의 이 진흙투성이 들판에서 만났다. 두 남자는 동갑이었고, 유럽이 앞날을 알 수 없는 상태에 놓여 있다는 것을 아는 대담한 군사 전략가들이었다.

두 군대는 아주 오랜 기간에 걸쳐 싸웠고, 마치 나폴레옹이 이길 것처럼 보였지만 웰링턴의 병사들에 결국 프로이센 군대가 합류했다. 나폴레옹의 병사들이 극복하기에는 너무 많았다. 이 프랑스 지도자는 패배해서 전쟁터를 떠났고, 이번에는 세인트 헬레나 섬으로 추방당했다. 아마도 그의 인생에서 처음으로 나폴레옹은 도망치려는 시도를 하지 않았고, 그의 지위를 되찾기 위한 공격 계획도 세우지 않았다. 그의 생에 마지막 몇 년 동안 그를 괴롭혔던 것은 아마도 복통이었을지도 모른다. 대부분의 역사학자는 이전 황제가 1821년에 위암으로 사망했다고 믿는다. 나폴레옹의 불굴의 정신

은 다시 부활하지 못하겠지만, 이 위대한 군사 지도자의 유산은 전 세계에서 보여지는 민주적인 이상들로 살아있다!

3장. 변화를 위한 저항가, 마하트마 간디

p.52~53

지도자들은 흔히 타고나는 것이지 만들어지는 게 아니라고 한다. 하지만 간디는 지도자로 시작하지 않았다. 정말로 그는 맨 처음부터 놀라움으로 가득했

다! 가난한 사람들의 대변자로 알려진 이 남자는 1869년에 유복한 가정에서 태어났다. 그는 상인 계급에서 편안하게 자랐다. 그의 아버지는 정부에서

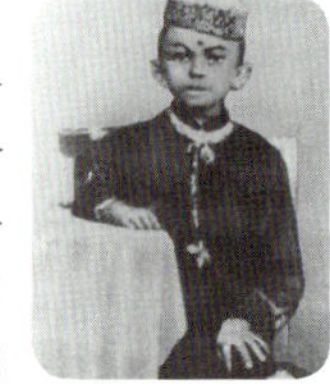

명망 있는 위치에 있었고, 간디는 영어를 배우는 좋은 학교들에 다닐 수 있었다. 그가 결혼한 때는 13세였는데, 심지어 더 놀라운 것은 그가 독실한 어머니의 힌두교에 대한 믿음을 거역하는 반항하는 십대였다는 사실이다.

p.54~55

간디는 어떻게 그의 삶을 변화시켰고, 나아가 변화를 위한 영웅적인 지도자가 되었을까? 몇 가지 사건이 간디에게 변화를 일으키는 영향을 주었지만, 그것들 중에 아마도 가장 놀라운 것은 인도인들을 도우려는 간디의 사명이 *남아프리카공화국*에 뿌리를 내렸었다는 것이다! 간디는 법정 변호사가 되기 위해 런던에서 공부한 다음에 인도로 되돌아왔지만, 봄베이에서 그는 아주 성공한 변호사는 아니었다. 그는 1893년에 남아프리카공화국으로 갈 기회를 덥석 잡았지만, 거기서 그가 맞닥뜨린 편견에 대한 대비가 안 되어 있었다.

양복을 입긴 했지만 간디는 터번도 썼다. 한 치안 판사가 그에게 머리에 쓴 것을 벗으라고 요구했지만 간디는 거부하고 법정을 나갔다. 그리고 후에, 제대로 갖춰 입고 일등석 표를 가지고 있었음에도, 그는 더 어두운 피부색 때문에 기차에서 쫓겨났다. 몹시 추운 날 밤을 역에서 보내게 된 간디의 시각은 완전히 바뀌었다. 그는 남아프리카공화국에 남기로 결심했고, 그가 목격했던 불의와 싸우기로 했다.

p.56~57

이 젊은 변호사는 인도 이민자들에 대한 차별적인 관행들을 없애기를 원했다. 기차 사건이 일어나고 몇 달이 지나지 않아, 간디는 나탈 인도인 회의를 설립했다. 그러는 동안에 전쟁의 씨앗들이 남아프리카 공화국에 퍼져가고 있었다. 1899년 보어 전쟁과 함께 간디는 인도인들이 정당성을 얻을 기회를 엿보았다. 만일 그들이 전쟁에서 복무한다면, 확실히 그들은 시민권을 취득할 수 있을 것이라고 그는 믿었다. 그는 300명의 자유 인도인과 800명의 도제살이로 들어갔거나 또는 계약된 노동자들로 인도인 야전 의무대를 조직했다. 이것은 부상당한 남아프리카공화국 흑인들을 돕기 위해 설립된 몇 개 안되는 의료부대 중 하나였고, 간디는 들것 운반부로 복무했다.

p.58~59

하지만 전쟁이 끝났을 때, 인도인의 상황은 나아지지 않았다. 사실, 인도인들은 훨씬 더 나쁘게 취급받았다. 1906년, 트란스발 정부는 모든 인도인에게 등록을 하라고 요구했다. 간디의 비폭력 시위의 사용은 간디가 신분 증명서를 가지고 다니기를 거부했을 때 시작되었다. 인도인들은 법에 저항할 때 평화적인 저항을 함으로써 그의 본보기를 따랐다. 이윽고 그들은 이 소극적 저항에 대한 대가를 치르기 시작했다. 인도인들은 태형을 받거나 총살을 당하거나, 수감되었다. 간디도 체포되었고, 그가 헨리 데이비드 소로의 〈시민 불복종〉을 읽었던 것은 1908년 감옥에서였다. 소로의 글은 비폭력 시위를 통한 시민 정의를 위한 그의 싸움에 훨씬 더 많은 영감을 주었다. 다음으로, 간디는 주로 광부들과 농장 노동자들인 노동자 계급의 인도인들에게 부과되는 세금에 대해 항의하는  파업을 요구했다. 1913년에 그는 2천 명 이상의 사람들을 이끌고 나탈에서 트란스발로 갔고, 비록 체

포되어 감옥에서 9개월을 복역했지만 간디의 노력은 보상을 받았다. 영국 정부는 세금을 낮췄고, 간디는 풀려났다. 아마도 더 중요하기로는, 간디의 시민 불복종과 소극적 저항의 방법들은 단지 남아프리카 공화국뿐만 아니라 영국과 인도에서도 성공했다는 것이다. 간디가 고향으로 돌아갈 때였다.

p.60~61

간디는 20여 년 이상 밖에 있다가 인도로 돌아왔고, 고국의 가난 때문에 행복하지 않았다. 1920년까지 그는 인도의 독립이 나라를 구하고, 국민의 삶을 향상시킬 수 있는 유일한 방법이라고 확신했다. 그는 주요 정치 정당인 인도 국민 회의(INC) 안에서 변화와 함께 개선을 위한 운동을 시작했다. 그러나 먼저, 간디는 개인적 변화를 만들었다. 그는 인도의 도티를 입기 시작했는데, 이 옷은 힌두교의 남자들이 입는 것으로 허리 부분에서 묶이게 되어 있다. 간디는  그의 정장을 대체한 이 하얀색 전통 의상을 그의 '애도 예복'이라고 불렀다. 그것은 인도의 가난한 사람들과 함께한다는 그의 연대, 또는 통합의 선언이었다. 그는 절대 다른 옷은 입지 않았다.

간디는 인도 국민 회의를 변화시키기 위해 끊임없이 일했다. 전에는 이것이 인도의 엘리트들을 위한 정당이었는데, 이들은 부유하고 상위의 카스트, 즉 사회적 계급이었다. 간디는 인도 국민 회의를 *모든* 국민에게로 가져왔다. 종교적인 신념이나 계급에 상관없이 그들은 모두 비폭력, 비타협 저항에 대한 생각을 품었다. 그리고 다른 무엇보다도 간디는 영국으로부터의 인도 독립을 원했다. 간디가 새로운 이름으로 불린 것은 이 시기 동안이었는데, '위대한 영혼'을 의미하는 칭호인 '마하트마'였다. 다른 사람들도 같은 칭호를 얻었지만, 누구도 마하트마 간디처럼 유명하진 않다!

p.62~63

불행하게도, 그에게 또 다른 체포를 가져온 것은 간디의 널리 퍼진 명성과 성공이었다. 왜냐하면, 그의

저항 운동이 점점 커졌기 때문에 영국 정부는 간디를 2년 동안 감옥에 가두었다. 그가 풀려났을 때, 인도인들은 여전히 영국의 통치하에서 고생하고 있었다. 그래서 간디는 다시 저항했다. 영국의 소금법은 인도인들이 소금을 팔거나 모으는 것을 금지했고, 더 심한 것은, 그들은 영국 소금에 과도한 세금을 내야 했다. 간디는 수천 명의 가난한 인도인들을 이끌고 그들이 바다로부터 소금을 끓이는 곳으로 소금 행진을 했다. 이 행동은 불법이었지만, 영국은 다양한 시민 불복종의 행동들뿐만 아니라 대규모 시위자들도 통제할 수 없었다. 영국은 항복했고, 간디는 런던으로 가서 공식 회담에서 인도 국민 회의를 대표했다.

결국, 그는 아주 오랫동안 애썼던 인도 독립을 얻는 데는 실패했다. 간디는 인도로 돌아와서 정치를 그만두겠다고 맹세했다. 하지만 그때 제2차 세계대전이 시작되었다. 윈스턴 처칠은 인도에게 전쟁에서 영국을 지원하라고 요구했지만, 간디는 그들이 여전히 영국 지배하에 있는 때에 인도인들이 영국을 위해서 싸워야 한다고 생각하지 않았다. 따라서 그의 다음 저항은 영국에게 영원히 '인도를 떠나라'고 요청하는 것이었다. 처칠은 물러서기를 거부했고, 간디와 그의 아내는 투옥되었다. 이번에는 저항이 나라 곳곳에서 일어나서 폭력적으로 변했다! 1944년, 간디는 마침내 풀려났지만, 슬프게도 그의 아내는 아직 감옥에 수감되어 있던 몇 달 전에 사망했다.

켰다! 이 두 나라 사이에 전쟁이 발발했다. 간디는 단식을 통해 그가 새로운 평화를 가져올 수 있기를 바라며 캘커타로 떠났다. 하지만 한 기도회에 가던 도중에 그는 가슴에 세 발의 총을 맞았다.

아마도 마하트마 간디의 삶 속의 모든 것 중에서 가장 놀라운 것은 그가 노벨평화상을 수상하지 못했다는 것이었다. 그는 1937년, 38년, 39년, 47년, 그리고 마지막으로 1948년에 후보에 올랐다. 간디가 왜 그 상을 결코 받지 못 했는가에 대한 많은 토론이 있었다. 요근래 몇 년 동안, 간디가 비록 강력한 비폭력 옹호자이긴 했지만 그의 시위들이 가끔 폭력으로 흘렀었다는 것이 가장 유력한 것으로 보인다. 슬프게도 이 사실이 그가 처음 네 번 후보자가 되었을 때, 불리했는지도 모른다. 하지만 1948년에는 간디가 마침내 수상할 것이 확실했다. 첫 번째로는 물론 간디를 포함해서 세 명의 이름만이 선발 후보자 명단에 있었기 때문이었다. 그리고 두 번째로 위원회에서 발표한 성명에 따르면,

노벨상은 '적합한 *살아 있는* 후보자가 없어서' 그 해에는 수여되지 않았다. 간디는 1948년 1월 30일에 암살되었었다. 그는 어떤 상도 받을 필요가 없었다. 그는 영원히 인도를 바꾼 변화들을 일으킬 정도로 충분히 오래 살았다. 그는 그의 가장 유명한 명언인 '당신이 바로 세상에서 보고자 하는 그 변화여야 한다!(세상을 변화시키고 싶다면 당신부터 변화된 삶을 살아야 한다!)'를 진실로 실천한 지도자였다.

p.64~65

간디는 마침내 인도의 독립을 이뤄냈지만, 이것은 그가 마음속에 그려왔던 독립은 아니었다. 하나에서 두 개의 나라가 생겨났다. 인도와 파키스탄이라는 이 나라들은 종교적 경계에 따라 나누어졌고, 비극적이게도 이것은 혼란과 폭력, 대량 살상을 일으

p.68~69

또 다른 위대한 지도자가 남아프리카공화국에서 나왔다. 그는 자신의 작은 마을의 자유를 떠나 다른 사람들이 자유로울 수 있도록 하기 위해 결국 수년 동안을 수감되어 지냈다. 그의 이름은 롤리랄라였는데,

세상은 그를 넬슨으로 더 잘 알고 있다.

넬슨 만델라는 1918년 남아프리카공화국에서 태어났는데, 템부족 사람들의 왕 대행에게 주요 고문 역할을 하던 이의 아들이었다. 그는 기독교 학교에 보내졌는데, 그곳에서 관습대로 넬슨이라는 기독교식 이름을 얻었다. 그러나 그가 겨우 아홉 살이었을 때, 그의 아버지가 사망했고, 넬슨은 이 청소년을 위한 계획을 가지고 있었던 템부족의 한 고위 인사에게 입양되었다. 그는 넬슨이 위대한 지도자가 되기를 원했다. 그리고 넬슨은 자기 나라에서의 불평등에 대해 더 많이 알아 갈수록, 국민들에게 위대한 변화들을 가져오는 지도자가 되겠다고 더욱 결심을 굳히게 되었다. 비록 젊은이였지만, 넬슨 만델라는 그의 한평생을 특징짓는 저항 정신을 보여주었다.

p.70~73

감리교 대학인 힐드타운을 졸업한 후에 그는 포트 하레 대학을 다녔는데, 그 대학은 남아프리카공화국에 있는 그 당시 고등 교육을 받으려고 하는 흑인들을 위한 유일한 기관이었다. 하지만 그는 대학 정책들에 항의하다가 퇴학당했다. 쫓겨난 이후에 그는 불명예스럽게 집으로 돌아왔고, 그의 후견인은 그의 결혼을 주선하기로 했다. 하지만 넬슨 만델라는 그의 부인을 스스로 선택하기를 원했고, 그래서 요하네스버그로 달아났다. 여전히 그는 부인을 찾는 일보다 더 많은 것들을 마음에 두고 있었다. 그는 통신 강좌를 통해 법을 공부했다. 그는 나중에 차별에 대한 투쟁에서 주요 인물들이 되는 많은 사람을 만났다. 그리고 그는 아프리카 민족 회의에 가담했다. 거기서 그는 새롭게 결성된 청년 동맹을 관리했다. 그러고 나서, 1948년에 국민당이 권력을 장악했다.

국민당이 남아프리카공화국에 아파르트헤이트 정책을 시작했을 때, 넬슨 만델라는 30세였다. 그것은 아주 거창한 단어는 아니었지만 남아

프리카공화국의 흑인들에게 막대한 영향을 미쳤다. 아파르트헤이트라는 이 제도는 인종에 따라 사람들을 강제적으로 분리하는 차별 정책을 장려했다. 그것은 또한 피부색을 근거로 하는 차별을 허용했다. 그래서 여러분이 만약 흑인 남아프리카공화국 사람이라면, 여러분의 권리는 심각하게 제한을 받았을 것이다.

p.72~73

머지않아 만델라와 아프리카 민족 회의는 대규모 시민 불복종의 형태로 행동을 취했다. 부당한 법에 대한 저항 운동으로, 만델라와 다른 사람들은 전국을 돌아다녔다. 그들은 시위들을 격려했고 사법 제도를 제압하려는 시도를 했다. 넬슨 만델라는 이 시기 동안에 유명해져서 그가 반역 혐의로 체포되었을 때

그렇게 놀랍지도 않았다. 5년 동안 재판이 계속되었는데, 보통 만델라는 밤에는 감옥에서 자고 낮에는 그의 법률 사무소에서 일하는 것이 허락되었다. 결국에 그와 다른 사람들은 무혐의로 풀려났으며, 만델라는 마침내 자유가 되었다. 하지만 샤프빌이 오고 있었다.

샤프빌은 트란스발에 있는 작은 흑인 거주 지역일 뿐이지만, 1960년에 그곳은 전 세계를 충격에 빠트린 대학살의 현장이었다. 69명의 아파르트헤이트를 반대하는 시위자들이 샤프빌 경찰서 밖에서 시위하던 중 죽임을 당했다. 혼란과 폭동이 온 나라를 휩쓸면서 정부는 아프리카 민족 회의를 금지했다. 평화로운 시위의 시기는 끝났다고 만델라와 그의 동료들은 생각했다. 그것은 '국민의 창'이라고 불렸던 아프리카 민족 회의의 군사적인 파당이 발전하게 되는 시작이었다.

p.74~75

이것은 또 만델라가 지하에 숨는 시작이었다. 그는 계속 세간의 이목을 피해서 숨어 지냈다. 하지만 동시에 국민의 창은 만델라의 말대로 정부가 '제정신'을 차리게 하려고 노력했다. 그들은 정부 건물들뿐만 아니라 철도 선로들도 폭파했다. 비록 그들이 목숨을 뺏는 정책을 가지고 있었던 것은 아니지만, 사고로 죽은 이들이 있었다. 몇 년 후에, 만델라는 국민의 창의 존재 이면에 있는 이유를 설명했다. "다른 모든 것이 실패했을 때였고, 평화로운 시위를 위한 모든 수단이 우리에게 금지되었을 때라서 정치적인 투쟁의 폭력적인 형태에 나선다는 결정을 할 수밖에 없었다."

1962년에 만델라가 붙잡혔고, 불법적으로 나라를 떠난 것을 이유로 수감되었다. 그 당시, 그는 5년형을 선고받았다. 하지만, 그가 투옥된 동안에 많은 아프리카 민족 회의 중진들이 요하네스버그의 교외 지역인

리보니아에서 잡혔다. 만델라는 다른 사람들과 연루되어 있었고, 리보니아 재판에서 그와 다른 동료들은 반역, 사보타주, 그리고 폭력 모의로 형을 선고받았다. 넬슨 만델라는 로벤 섬에 수감되어 그다음 27년을 보내게 되었다.

p.76~77

그는 아주 작은 감방에서 혼자 지냈고, 종종 화장실도 없고 제대로 된 침대도 없는 독방 감금을 당했다. 그는 또 해가 뜰 때부터 해가 질 때까지 돌을 부수며 채석장에서도 일했다. 정부는 만델라를 무너뜨리고 그에게 굴욕감을 줌으로써 그의 추종자들을 흩어지게 하고 싶어 했다. 하지만 만델라는 교도소 감방 안에서도 계속해서 항의했다. 그때, 국제사회가 밖에서 그를 위한 지지를 모으기 시작했다. 예를 들어, 1964년에 남아프리카공화국은 올림픽 출전이 금지

되었고 경제적 제재도 유지됐다. 70년대에 만델라는 그의 자서전인 〈자유를 향한 머나먼 여정〉뿐만 아니라 대량의 정치적인 성명서도 몰래 반출했다. 비록 1995년까지 세계의 나머지 나라에서는 출간되지 않았지만, 남아프리카공화국에서는 많은 사람이 그의 글을 읽었다. 그럼에도 불구하고 이 사람들은 남아프리카공화국에서 아파르트헤이트 반대로 알려진 이 남자, 넬슨 만델라가 어떻게 생겼는지 몰랐다. 그의 사진들을 인쇄하는 것은 불법이었던 것이다!

1980년, *프리 넬슨 만델라* 운동이 남아프리카공화

국의 가장 유명한 정치 죄수를 석방하라는 압력을 가하기 시작했다. 국제적으로 알려진 음악인들이 만델라를 지지하며 모였을 때인 그의 70번째 생일을 위한 음악 콘서트와 같은 큰 행사들이 있었다. 그리고 나라 안에서는 인종 차별주의 정권에 대항하는 폭력이 커지고 있었다. 그리고 또 10년이 흘러갔다. 하지만 1990년 2월 11일, 넬슨 만델라는 마침내 감옥에서 풀려났다. 아파르트헤이트 법들은 당시 FW(프레데리크 빌렘) 데 클레르크 대통령에 의해 폐지되었다.

p.78~79

놀랄 것도 없이 아파르트헤이트의 종말은 쉽지 않았다. 갈등과 긴장이 당시를 지배했지만 만델라는 조용히 결의하고, 남아프리카공화국에서의 화해를 위해 끊임없이 노력했다. 1993년, 넬슨 만델라와 FW

데 클레르크는 나라를 치유하기 위한 노력으로 노벨평화상을 받았다. 그리고 1994년에 남아프리카공화국이 최초의 다인종 총선거를 치렀을 때, 넬슨 만델라가 최초의 흑인 대통령이 되었다. 넬슨 만델라는 대통령으로서 많은 일을 이뤄냈다. 그는 남아프리카공화국 흑인들의 삶을 향상시킬 수 있는 사회·경제적 프로

그램들을 도입했다. 백인을 포함해서 소수에 대한 차별을 금지하는 새 헌법이 제정되었다. 그는 통합된 남아프리카공화국이라는 목표를 향해 일했다. 그는 흑인들이 예전의 악행들에 대해 보복하려는 것을 막고, 대신에 모두의 평화로운 통합을 격려했다.

넬슨 만델라의 대통령 임기가 1999년에 끝나고 2004년에 정계를 은퇴한 후에도 그는 계속해서 국민을 이끌었다. 만델라는 사회 정의와 평화를 위해 일했다. 그는 넬슨 만델라 재단과 엘더스를 설립했는데, 이 기관들은 단지 남아프리카공화국에서 뿐만 아니라 전  세계적으로 사람들이 겪고 있는 고통을 종식시키는 데 헌신했다. 넬슨 만델라는 2013년에 95세의 나이로 사망했는데, 그는 교도소 감방이 나라의 자유를 향한 그의 꿈을 가두는 것을 거부한 사람이었다!

5장. 캘커타의 성인, 마더 테레사

p.82~83

마더 테레사는 왜소했을지 모르지만, 그것이 결코 그녀로 하여금 큰일들을 하는 것을 막지는 못했다. 아마도 그녀의 가장 유명한 말 중 하나는 심지어 그녀의 작은 키에 의해 영감을 받은 것이었을지 모른다. 그녀는 자주 말했다. "우리 모두가 위대한 일을 할 수 있는 것은 아니다. 하지만 우리는 위대한 사랑으로 작은 일들을 할 수 있다." 마더 테레사는 보통 파란색과 흰색으로 된  사리를 입은 모습으로 사진에 나오는데, 그것은 사랑의 선교수녀회의 드레스처럼 생긴 소박한 유니폼이

다. 하지만 그녀는 그 유명한 수녀회를 꾸리기 훨씬 이전부터 수녀였다. 아녜즈 곤제 보야지우라는 이름의 여학생에서 캘커타의 성인 테레사가 되기까지의 여정은 길었고, 그녀를 전 세계로 데려다주는 데에는 우여곡절로 가득차 있었다!

p.84~85

그녀의 여정은 선교사가 되려고 고향인 마케도니아공화국의 스코페를 떠나 아일랜드의 로레토 수녀회에 들어가면서 시작되었다. 하지만 처음에 그녀는 인도에서 가르칠 수 있게 영어를 배워야 했다. 그녀는 열심히 공부했고, 막 19세가 되었을 때, 히말라야 산맥 근처의 다질링으로 가서 세인트 테레사 학교에서 가르치기 시작했다. 오늘날 이렇게 전 세계적인 인지도를 얻게 된 이름을 그녀가 선택하게 된 것이 바로 여기에서였다. 수녀원에서 공부하는 젊은 여자들은 수녀가 되기 전에 일련의 서약들을 한다. 젊은 아녜즈는 첫번째 종교적인 서약을 할 때, 예수의 작은 꽃으로도 알려진 리지외의 성녀 테레즈라는 이름을 원했다. 하지만 다른 수녀가 이미 그 이름을 가지고 있었기 때문에 그녀는 테레즈라는 이름을 가질 수 없었다. 그래서 그녀는 대신에 테레사라는 스페인식 철자를 선택했다. 그녀가 1937년에 그녀의 마지막 서약을 했을 때, 그녀는 관례대로 '마더'라는 칭호를 얻게 되었고, 그때부터 마더 테레사로 알려지게 되었다.

마더 테레사는 다음으로 세인트 메리 여자고등학교에서 가르쳤는데, 이 학교는 캘커타에 있는 가장 가난한 이들 중 일부를 보살폈다. 교육을 통해 그녀는 이 벵골 소녀들의 고통을 덜어주기를 바랐다. 마더 테레사는 심지어 그녀의 어린 학생들과 더 잘 의사

소통하기 위해서 벵골어와 힌디어를 말하는 것을 배웠다. 1944년에 그녀는 그 학교의 교장이 되었고, 비록 그녀는 그 도시에서 목격했던 가난, 기근, 폭력, 그리고 절망에 괴로워하긴 했지만 마치 마더 테레사의 봉사하는 삶은 완성된 것처럼 보였다. 하지만 그때 그녀는 그녀가 '부르심 속의 부르심'이라고 묘사했던 것을 경험했다.

그것은 1946년이었고, 마더 테레사가 기차를 타고 피정하기 위해 가는 중이었는데, 그녀는 그리스도가 그녀에게 말하는 소리를 들었다. 그리스도는 그녀에게 학교를 떠나 캘커타의 빈민가에 있는, 그 도시에서 가장 가난한 사람들 사이로 가서 일해야 한다고 말했다. 그녀는 거의 40세였고, 비록 그녀가 가게 해 달라고 수녀원을 설득하는 데 거의 2년이 걸렸지만 그녀는 그녀의 소명에 대해서는 의심하지 않았다. 그리고 그녀가 떠나도 된다는 허가를 받았을 때 조차도 마더 테레사는 그녀가 무엇을 해야 하는지 분명한 생각을 갖고 있지는 못했다. 그녀는 그녀의 수녀복을 하얀색과 파란색으로 된 사리로 바꿨고, 다음 여섯 달 동안 기초 의료 훈련을 공부하겠다고 결정했다. 그러고 나서 그녀는 빈민가로 들어갔는데, 그녀의 유일한 바람은 캘커타의 '최빈곤층'의 고통을 덜어주는 것이었다.

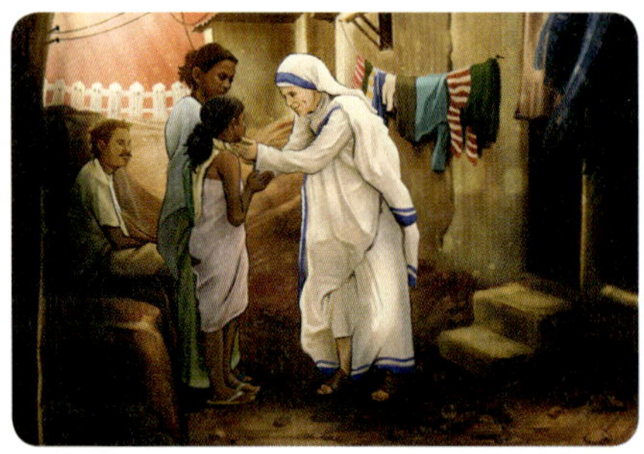

그것은 쉬운 일이 아니었고, 마더 테레사는 여러 번 예전 수녀원의 안락함으로 돌아가기를 간절히 바랐다. 하지만 그녀가 스스로 식량과 물자를 구걸해야 했을 때조차도 그녀는 포기하기를 거부했다. 그녀는 빈민가에 학교를 열었고, 죽어가는 사람들과 가난한 사람들을 위한 시설도 세웠다. 1950년에 마침내 그

녀는 바티칸으로부터 그녀가 사랑의 선교수녀회라고 부르는 수녀회를 허가받았다. 그곳은 단 몇 명의 여자들로 구성된 작은 단체였는데, 대부분이 마더 테레사가 있던 전 고등학교인 세인트 메리 학교 출신의 학생들과 선생님들이었다. 하지만 이 작은 시작은 마더 테레사가 상상할 수 있었던 것보다 더 크게 성장했다!

그녀와 그녀의 수녀들은 전 세계 수천 수만 명의 사람들에게 도움을 주었다. 그녀의 말로는 그들은 '굶주린 사람들, 헐벗은 사람들, 집이 없는 사람들, 장애가 있는 사람들, 앞을 못 보는 사람들, 나환자들, 사회 전체적으로 환영받지 못하고, 사랑받지 못하고, 보살핌을 받지 못한다고 느끼는 모든 사람, 사회에 짐이 되거나 모두에게서 배척당하는 사람들'을 보살폈다. 이 포교단은 고아원, 에이즈 환자들을 위한 호스피스, 난민들을 위한 구조, 나환자들을 위한 격리 시설, 그리고 이동 진료소들도 되었다. 그녀의 자비로운 활동은 주의를 끌었고, 곧 기부가 쏟아져서 마더 테레사는 캘커타 훨씬 너머로 시설과 도움을 제공할 수 있었다.

그녀의 포교단이 커짐에 따라 점점 더 많은 자매가 그녀에게 합류했다. 그녀의 수녀들은 가난한 사람들을 돕기 위해 아시아, 남북 아메리카, 유럽, 그리고 아프리카로 갔다. 그리고 그들이 어디를 가든, 그들이 봉사하는 사람들의 신앙 안에서 도움을 주었다. 힌두교도이든 무슬림이든, 무신론자이든 가톨릭 신자이든, 사랑의 선교수녀회에게는 차이가 없었다. 곧, 수녀들에게 사랑의 선교형제회와 많은 평신도 자원봉사자들이 합류했다. 그녀는 인도의 보석이라는 상을 받았는데, 이 상은 인도 시민이 받을 수 있는 최고의 영예이다. 1979년에 마더 테레사는 '고통

을 겪고 있는 인류에게 도움을 준' 공로로 노벨 평화상을 받았다.

p.90~91

수년 동안 건강이 나빴음에도 불구하고, 마더 테레사는 계속해서 수녀들을 이끌고 전 세계를 돌며 가난한 사람들과 죽어가는 이들을 위해 봉사했다. 하지만 1997년 9월 5일, 이 자그마한 수녀의 큰 심장이 마  침내 멈췄다. 그럼에도 불구하고 마더 테레사의 이야기가 끝난 것은 아니었다. 그녀의 긴 여정 동안에는 예상 밖의 한두 가지 또 다른 일이 있었다. 그녀의 사후, 마더 테레사의 일기 글이 공개되었고, 글에서 그녀는 자주 그녀의 믿음에 대한 의구심을 표현

 했다. 하지만 사람들은 믿음을 잃는 대신에 영감을 얻었다! 마더 테레사의 의구심들은 오로지 그녀가 봉사했던 평범한 사람들과의 강한 유대 관계를 입증하는 것이었고, 이러한 유대 관계는 결국 그녀를 성인으로 이끌었다!

p.92~93

살아 있을 때와 같이 사후에도 마더 테레사는 아픈 사람들과 고통받는 사람들에게 도움을 주었다. 2002년, 로마 가톨릭 교회의 수장인 바티칸은 1998년에 마더 테레사의 덕분이라는 첫 번째 기적을 인정했다. 인도의 한 여성은 마더 테레사의 도움을 청하는 기도를 한 다음에 종양이 치료되었다. 13년 후에 프란치스코 교황은 바이러스성 뇌 감염이 있던 한 브라질 남자의 가족이 마더 테레사에게 기도한 이후인 2008년에 그가 치료되자 마더 테레사의 두 번째 기적을 인정했다. 2016년 9월 4일, 수천 수만 명의 사람이 가난한 사람들에게 한 일 때문에 '빈민굴의 성인'으로 불리는 이 여인의 시성식에 참석하

기 위해 로마에 모였다. 오늘날 그녀는 캘커타의 성인 테레사로 알려져 있는데, 이 성인은 위대한 사랑으로 위대한 일들을 했다!

여러분은 이 페이지들 사이에서 위대한 지도자의 자질들을 모두 발견했는가? 연민, 용기, 독창성, 그리고 불굴의 의지는 그 자질들 중 몇 가지이다, 그렇지 않은가? 아마도 여러분은 빅토리아 여왕, 나폴레옹, 간디, 넬슨 만델라, 그리고 심지어 마더 테레사로부터 훨씬 더 많은 특징을 말할 수 있을지 모른다. 하지만 한 가지는 분명하다. 이 남녀들은 세상을 변화시  키기 위해 시작하지 않았다. 그들은 강력한 요구를 보았고 그들이 어떤 차이를 만들어 낼 지를 인식하지 못한 채 행동했다. 여러분 역시 위대한 리더십의 자질들을 발전시킬 수 있고, *여러분*이 세상 속에서 어떤 차이를 만들 수도 있을지 누가 알겠는가!

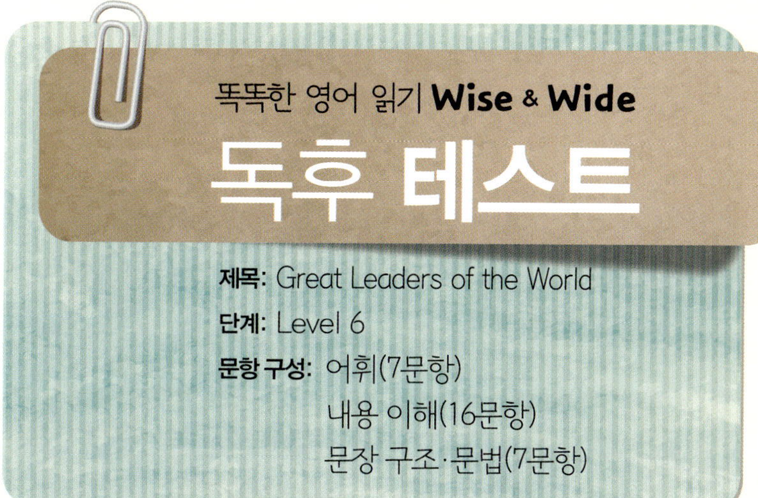

제목: Great Leaders of the World

단계: Level 6

문항 구성: 어휘(7문항)

내용 이해(16문항)

문장 구조·문법(7문항)

❖ 독후 테스트는 홈페이지(www.darakwon.co.kr)에서 온라인으로도 풀어보실 수 있습니다.
이 경우 점수와 응시 결과에 대한 평가까지 확인하실 수 있습니다.
추가로 제공되는 단어 퀴즈도 풀어보세요.

1. Which of the following pair has the wrong past tense form of the verb?
    ① set − set
    ② put − put
    ③ flee − flee
    ④ spread − spread

2. Which of the following is NOT a word represents a person?
    ① pioneer
    ② trailblazer
    ③ squalor
    ④ vendor

3. Which of the following is similar to the word "transform"?
    ① build
    ② change
    ③ travel
    ④ carry

※ Choose the right word for each blank. (4~5)

4.
> 빅토리아는 가난한 사람들의 고통을 덜어주는 여러 개혁들을 책임지고 있었다.
> → Victoria was responsible ___________ many reforms that eased the suffering of the poor.

    ① at   ② of
    ③ for   ④ with

5.

> 그 집정부는 3명의 통령으로 교체됐고, 나폴레옹이 제1통령이 되었다.
>
> → The Directory was replaced ____________ a three-member consulate, and Napoleon became first consul.

① up   ② of
③ into   ④ with

※ Choose the common word for the two blanks. (6~7)

6.

> • Her beloved husband, Albert, died ________ typhoid fever in December of 1861.
> • Napoleon knew the people were tired ________ civil wars and the chaos in their country.

① of   ② for
③ with   ④ into

7.

> • In 1863, in fact, the railways and the London Underground were built, thanks ________ her support.
> • She was unable ________ give him an heir.

① on   ② of
③ to   ④ against

8. What happened in 1840 that changed how Queen Victoria ruled?
   ① Victoria's mother died.
   ② Lord Melbourne was no longer prime minister.
   ③ Victoria married Prince Albert.
   ④ Victoria married an Italian prince.

9. What was the Great Exhibition sometimes called?
   ① Albert and Victoria's Exhibition
   ② the Crystal Palace Exhibition
   ③ the Mighty Museum Exhibition
   ④ the Crystal Museum Exhibition

10. What was said when the monarchy doubled in size during Victoria's reign?
   ① The sun rises and sets in England.
   ② The sun never sets on the British Empire.
   ③ The sun and moon reign in Britain.
   ④ The sun always sets in the east of England.

11. What was Napoleon working toward in Corsica, in 1789?
   ① He was attending school in France.
   ② He was hoping to free the island of French rule.
   ③ He was in his homeland, applying for a government position.
   ④ He was in Paris, studying military strategy.

12. Which of the following was NOT a reform that Napoleon brought to France?
   ① an improved Constitution of the Republic
   ② an end to the feudal system
   ③ a new banking system
   ④ an improved water and sewage system

13. Why did the Napoleonic Code spread throughout the world?

① People asked Napoleon to share his ideals.

② Napoleon brought his code to the countries he conquered.

③ The code was easy to understand since it was written in English.

④ Everyone who heard about the code wanted it, too.

14. Why was it odd that Napoleon would crown himself Emperor of France?

① He believed in the ideals of the Revolution, including equality.

② He had never liked the idea of royalty.

③ He was not ambitious at all and did not want to rule.

④ He was born on Corsica and was not a native-born Frenchman.

15. What was the result of Gandhi's call for a strike in 1913?

① The government forced Gandhi out of South Africa.

② Though he was imprisoned, a tax was dropped.

③ It became obvious that passive resistance didn't work.

④ Taxes were raised even higher and Indians were flogged.

16. Why was the Nobel Peace Prize NOT awarded in 1948?

① There was "no suitable living candidate."

② There were too many candidates on the short list.

③ There was no money to give to the winner.

④ The committee could not award the prize during a war.

17. Which quote is Gandhi most famous for?
    ① "You must be the man you wish to be in the world."
    ② "You must quit India or die."
    ③ "You must be the change that you wish to see in the world."
    ④ "You must always try to do your best every day."

18. What was Mandela arrested for during the Rivonia Trial?
    ① treason, violent conspiracy, and arson
    ② sabotage, arson, and murder
    ③ treason, sabotage, and violent conspiracy
    ④ murder, treason, and lying

19. What is the title of Mandela's autobiography?
    ① *Long Walk of Protest*
    ② *27 Years in Prison*
    ③ *Long Walk To Freedom*
    ④ *Protesting for Freedom*

20. Who was the first black President of South Africa?
    ① FW de Klerk
    ② Winnie Mandela
    ③ Nelson Mandela
    ④ William de Klerk

21. Why did Mother Teresa go to the Republic of Ireland?
① She joined the Sisters of Loreto to become a nurse.
② She joined a convent there to learn about computers.
③ She was ready to see the world and learn English.
④ She joined a convent to become a missionary.

22. Who were some of those that Mother Teresa and her nuns served?
① the criminals, the rich, and the doctors
② people who could pay for assistance
③ the crippled, the blind, the lepers
④ men who lived in the suburbs of India

23. What did the Vatican recognize so that Mother Teresa could be canonized?
① evidence of miracles
② proof of magic
③ evidence of wealth
④ kindness

※ Choose the wrong part of each sentence. (24~26)

24.
> 딱 한 사람의 이름만 대는 것은 정말로 어려울 것이다.
> → That would indeed be difficult to name just one.
>   ①   ② ③   ④

25.

그가 제대로 갖춰 입고 일등석 표를 가지고 있었음에도 불구하고, 그는 기차에서 쫓겨났다.

→ Even if he was well dressed and had a first class ticket, he was
　　　①　　　　　　　　　　　②　　　③

thrown off a train.
　　　　④

26.

그래서 그는 섬으로 돌아와 전략을 공부하면서 시간을 보냈다.

→ And so he returned to the island, spending his time study strategy.
　　　①　　　　　　②　　　　　　③　　　　　　　　④

※ Choose the common word for the blanks. (27~28)

27.

그들은 굶주린 사람들, 헐벗은 사람들, 집이 없는 사람들, 장애가 있는 사람들, 그리고 앞을 못 보는 사람들을 보살폈다.

→ They cared for _________ hungry, _________ naked, _________ homeless, _________ crippled, and _________ blind.

① a　　　　　　　　　　　　② the
③ people　　　　　　　　　　④ many

28.

넬슨이 자기 나라에서의 불평등에 대해 더 많이 알아 갈수록, 그는 지도자가 되어야겠다고 더 결심을 굳혔다.

→ The _________ Nelson learned about the inequalities in his country, the _________ he was determined to be a leader.

① better　　　　　　　　　② much
③ many　　　　　　　　　　④ more

※ Choose each correct sentence that is translated into English. (29~30)

29.

① But for February 11th, in 1990, Nelson Mandela was finally released from prison.

② But on February 11th, in 1990, Nelson Mandela was finally released from prison.

③ But from February 11th, in 1990, Nelson Mandela finally released from prison.

④ But at February 11th, in 1990, Nelson Mandela finally released from prison.

30.

① She was a great benefactor, provides not only her influence and funds.

② She was a great benefactor, providing not her influence but funds, too.

③ She was a great benefactor, provided not only her influence but also funds.

④ She was a great benefactor, providing not only her influence but funds, too.

Memo

Memo

Cathy C. Hall 선생님은…

방송 관련 학위를 받으신 후 라디오 뉴스 리포터와 광고 카피라이터로 일하시다가 대학으로 돌아가 영어 교사 자격증을
취득하셨습니다. 10년간 교직에 계시며 유치원생부터 고등학생까지 두루 가르치셨습니다. 현재는 어린이와 어른들을
위한 스토리, 에세이, 시를 집필하는 작가로 활동하십니다. Uncle John's Facts To Annoy Your Teacher, Chicken
Soup for the Soul's Think Positive for Kids, Cup of Comfort for Dog Lovers 등의 작품집에 작품을 발표하셨습니다.

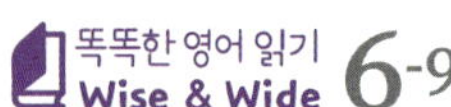

똑똑한 영어 읽기
Wise & Wide 6-9

세계의 위대한 지도자들
Great Leaders of the World

지은이 Cathy C. Hall
펴낸이 정규도

초판 1쇄 인쇄 2017년 7월 7일
초판 1쇄 발행 2017년 7월 14일

편집장 최주연
책임편집 장경희, 박지영
표지·본문 디자인 이은희
전산편집 이은희
일러스트 김연조
번역 김지은

다락원 경기도 파주시 문발로 211
내용문의 (02)736-2031 내선 510
구입문의 (02)736-2031 내선 250~252
Fax (02)732-2037
출판등록 1977년 9월 16일 제300-1977-23호
Copyright © 2017, 다락원

저자 및 출판사의 허락 없이 이 책의 일부 또는 전부를 무단 복제·전재·
발췌할 수 없습니다. 구입 후 철회는 회사 내규에 부합하는 경우에 가능하
므로 구입문의처에 문의하시기 바랍니다. 분실·파손 등에 따른 소비자 피
해에 대해서는 공정거래위원회에서 고시한 소비자 분쟁 해결 기준에 따라
보상 가능합니다. 잘못된 책은 바꿔 드립니다.

ISBN 978-89-277-0430-0 18740 / 978-89-277-0371-6 18740(set)

http://www.darakwon.co.kr
다락원 홈페이지를 방문하시면 상세한 출판 정보와 함께 MP3 자료 등 다양한
어학 정보를 얻으실 수 있습니다.